Cicada Summer

Cicada
Summer

A Novel

Erica
McKeen

W. W. NORTON & COMPANY
Independent Publishers Since 1923

Canada Council   Conseil des arts
for the Arts   du Canada

We acknowledge the support of the Canada Council for the Arts

For information about permission to reproduce selections from this book,
write to Permissions, W. W. Norton & Company, Inc.,
500 Fifth Avenue, New York, NY 10110

For information about special discounts for bulk purchases, please
contact W. W. Norton Special Sales at specialsales@wwnorton.com or
800-233-4830

Manufacturing by Lakeside Book Company
Book design by Lovedog Studio
Production manager: Lauren Abbate

ISBN 978-1-324-07381-9 (pbk)

W. W. Norton & Company, Inc., 500 Fifth Avenue, New York, N.Y. 10110
www.wwnorton.com

W. W. Norton & Company Ltd., 15 Carlisle Street, London W1D 3BS

1 2 3 4 5 6 7 8 9 0

For Joan and Ann,
my grandmothers

A novel is a mirror
walking down a road.

—Michael Ondaatje,
The English Patient

(This is not a novel.)

Contents

Introduction

IF YOU FIND THIS BOOK, you are Husha. You are quiet and you can't speak. If you read this book, your tongue is husha, swollen in your mouth. Your lips are sewn together, there is an attic inside your head, mushrooms under your fingernails, a wide hole opening in front of your front door. Quiet down. Close your eyes, all of them. Read the carvings on the backs of your teeth with the soft hug of your throat. Swallow me.

If you find this book, you are Husha. If you are Husha, then you have found this book. If you are Husha, then you have written this book, your mother has written this book. This is not my book, it never was, it's Husha's, it's Husha's mother's and Nellie's and Arthur's. If you are Husha, then you remembered these stories before I dreamt them, and took part in the dreaming. And licked them clean like an animal cleans its young. And kept a furball inside you that hurts in your belly like felted cotton.

If you are Husha, then your mouth is full of cotton. Squeaks and numb wonderings of cotton.

If this book finds you, it's Husha looking out against the glass as you part your hair, back turned to the mirror.

Part One

Stasis

(Cereal)

HUSHA SITS IN SILENCE ON THE BED, a clock ticks high up on the wall behind her, them, she breathes, and behind the window in the outside is a black stillness, the cicadas have fallen out of movement and therefore out of sound. A clock ticks high up on the wall behind her, them, because she is in her grandfather's house, an anachronistic place that still has ticking clocks on walls. Husha sits in silence because her name requires it; her name is Husha because she sits in silence. When the cicadas started in early summer, grating like violin strings rubbed out of tune, her grandfather explained that cicadas are named after their sound.

Their name itself is noise, he told her. It comes from the Latin, also *cicada*. It's onomatopoeia, a word that's a sound.

All words are sounds, said Husha.

This word is primarily a sound, he said. Primordially. Cicadas are named after the sound of their song: *ci-ca-da*. If I named you that way—

You didn't name me.

He raised his eyebrows over the reflection of her in his glasses.

My mother named me, she wanted to say. She wanted them both to think of her mother, his daughter, found herself still vehement with the fact of her mother's death, wanted to stick this fact places like a knife, make her grandfather flinch as if he were biting down on a rotting tooth, wanted to uproot something rotten between the two of them. Uproot this dead woman crouching between them. She waited and he raised his eyebrows higher, maybe curious, maybe disapproving, maybe merely thoughtful and preoccupied, separate from her behind his watery eyes, following a line of thinking that he more and more, with age, struggled to maintain. As a younger man, he had been a professor, a scholar of plant pathology at the University of Western Ontario. Sometimes he still spoke as if he were conducting a lecture. Sometimes, an even more aggravating habit to Husha, who had just left graduate school, he spoke as if she had entered his office seeking advice. He spoke with crisp consonants, his tongue paper, a dictionary.

Over the reflection of her in his glasses, he raised his eyebrows.

If I were to name you, and I named you that way, he went on, I would name you the opposite of song, the spoken equivalent of silence.

What would that be? she asked. *It's a paradox*, she thought, not saying it because she knew he already knew.

He looked at her.

Husha, he said finally. Something like Husha.

But that's a bidding to silence, she said. That's a plea.

He shrugged, rolling his shoulders back into the armchair. Just as well.

Just as well, Husha sits in silence on the bed, as close as she can get to silence—a clock ticks high up on the wall behind her, them, they breathe. She sits in the gap made by Nellie's open legs, hooking her arms around Nellie's thighs, leaning back into Nellie's warm chest, Nellie who has just arrived that morning to the house, who sits in silence between Husha leaning back against her and the headboard pushing hard against her spine. Nellie holds Husha's shoulders in her hands and tries to hold the silence inside of her like holding her breath. Already she can feel the laughter coming, remembering that morning when she arrived and admitted she was hungry after traveling through the night and Husha poured her cereal in the kitchen while Husha's grandfather eyed her from his lumpy seat in the living room, saying nothing. And in her bowl when she bent to put the first spoonful into her mouth, stuck in the clump of cereal and half-submerged in milk, was a dead cicada. Its wings were splayed, transparent, a black network of veins. Husha saw and said, Oh God, oh no, I'm sorry, those damn cicadas, they get everywhere, they get into everything. Nellie sits and holds Husha and imagines eating the bug by accident, what that would have meant on their first morning, imagines picking its legs from between her teeth.

In the Cicada Summer

THE SUMMER HUSHA'S MOTHER DIED and Husha found this book, she went to live with her grandfather, Arthur, in the northern reaches of Southern Ontario. It was the summer after she graduated from her master's program, and she called it the Cicada Summer because that's how she wanted to remember it—in noise, the sound of the cicadas screeching from the trees, a white sustained vibration in her ears. She didn't want to remember the summer in images (her mother's neck skin sagging against the silver steel of the coroner's table; her grandfather hunched on the bathroom floor, having missed the toilet; the shadow of mold behind faucets and under the rim of countertops); or taste (the sour pickle sting of ONroute burgers, the muck before rain off the lake on the back of her tongue); or smell (her grandfather's coffee breath blooming out from his sleeping figure in the armchair, the musty swell of the cellar stairs, the super-sweet aroma of pansies and crocuses and lilies in the funeral-home parlor); or touch (but this she wouldn't elaborate on, not yet). She would rather call it the Cicada Summer than the Heatwave Summer, the Pandemic Summer, the summer she lost her mother, the summer of riots down in the States, the summer Canada craned over its shoulder at the looming US election as if groping for an unreachable itch, the summer smoke from the wildfires in California and Washington drifted across the continent and rubbed the sun red for two days. She would rather call it the Cicada Summer. Or maybe the Summer When Nellie Came.

8

When Nellie Came

THE MORNING THAT NELLIE ARRIVES, during the Cicada Summer, Husha is outside on the front porch gnawing the stringy fruit from a peach pit. It's hot, and a line of sweat traces her throat and disappears into the collar of her shirt. The taste of peach fruit is warm and sweet on the soft flesh beneath her tongue. Up above the house, between the treetops, a bird slices a line across the sun. The smoke has yet to come, so the sun is still silver in its halo when she closes her eyes to catch its edges against the underside of her eyelids. The morning Nellie arrives, Husha's mother has already died. This is how Husha's life will always be divided: the before and the after of her mother dying. Nellie arrives in the after, at the time in which Husha has once again remembered—like dreaming an old dream she had forgotten—how to eat a peach in sunlight on a front porch and suck tentacles of fruit from its pit and catch an impression of light with the skin around her eyes.

But still occasionally during this time in which she remembers the joy and sticky slick of fruit around her lips, she will blunder—still isn't woken all the way to this dream—as now, when she puts her teeth against the peach pit, she knows suddenly that it's not a pit but the shell of a cicada that has fallen from the trees. Somehow, the empty exoskeleton of a cicada has unhooked from the bark of one of those trees and fallen, made its way down through the humid air and into her hand and now into her mouth. She pauses with the bug in a kiss, the moment before it passes her lips and teeth—she imagines the crunch, wings against her throat reminding her inexplicably of the peanut butter toast she was eating when she received the call saying her mother had died—and her first unforgivable thought, *Thank God*, linked forever now with the taste of peanut butter. And wouldn't the empty inside of a cicada, the air trapped dark like a shadow there, taste just like that peanut butter?

She thinks about the crunch. She thinks about it but doesn't proceed, draws the bug away and sees that it's still a peach pit, ribbed and shiny.

Still sometimes she blunders.

Still sometimes her mother comes rocketing like a dead cicada into her throat.

In the driveway, where the sound of her shoes against the gravel has been masked by the buzz of cicadas in the trees (the buzz of the phone in Husha's hand, the peanut butter toast half-swallowed), Nellie stands and watches her old friend ring the peach pit with her lips and waits for the look, the looking up, that will touch like a grip is a touch in the night after nightmare, in the smoky unfiltering of the terror of night mirage. After this, in the after, if it can be called touch, this look across the length of the driveway.

* * * *

HUSHA SCRAMBLES across the kitchen counter, her grandfather watching from the living room, not saying anything, and snatches the cereal bowl out from between Nellie's hands.

Oh God, oh no, she says, I'm sorry, those damn cicadas, they get everywhere, they get into everything.

* * * *

SHE'LL BE staying with us, then? asks Arthur as Husha helps him into bed.

Afraid so, says Husha. She thinks of Nellie standing in the driveway with dust around her shoes and sweat in her hairline, her plaid shirt and heavy backpack and hangdog expression. Lips drooping in what might have been mock subjugation. After everything, after her absence, what could she say? The last time Husha had seen Nellie, they were sitting in an empty university classroom with their supervising professor, receiving training on how to conduct office hours via Zoom video chat. Nellie had saluted Husha and the professor on her way out the door. *Roger that, Sarge.* Then nothing. No phone calls, no response to Husha's text messages, radio-silent. Husha hadn't been surprised, not even disappointed. She didn't feel much during those first weeks of the pandemic—lockdown softened the edges of experience, made the days fuzzy, her bones buttery—and it's not like she hadn't known all along that Nellie might disappear, that she wasn't good at sticking around.

Husha pulls the blankets over the woolen socks that cover her grandfather's feet. Yeah, she repeats. I guess she's staying.

This house in cottage country, three hours to the northeast of Toronto, is her grandfather's house—he owns it in the language of legal documents and so should have the final word on who stays and who doesn't. But the house was also at one time Husha's grandmother's as much as it was her grandfather's, and at one time it was her mother's summer house as a little girl, and during holidays it was Husha's when she came with her mother to visit, and plenty of dogs and cats that came and went might have called it their own if they'd had the chance, and the land—which still feels the gravity of the Anishinaabe People's original territories—of course has its own opinion. Arthur, having had a father who cared too much for possession, is determined to not possess anything. He has never fully believed that he owned even his own skeleton. That's why, the morning that Nellie arrived, he watched from his lumpy seat in the living room and didn't say anything, not seeing it as his place to protest, not wanting to make his granddaughter uncomfortable as she measures his comfort in the number of fluffed pillows behind his head.

How long? he asks. By which he means, How many loaves of bread will we be buying now? Should we mark the need for an extra onion on the fridge grocery list?

Husha smiles and smooths the skin along his forehead with her hand. The skin is dewy and warm, and when she lifts her fingers to her face afterward she smells copper, salt. Nellie, taking her earrings out in the other room and listening to the murmurings through the wall—and who three weeks from now will help Husha's grandfather into the bath and make Husha think the same thing Nellie does now, Husha standing in the doorway while Nellie tests the water with the back of her hand—Nellie now with her earrings in her hands thinks that what occurs in the room adjacent to hers is a microcosmic moment always passing, always just there beyond the fingertips. An infinitesimal rebellion taking place in this exchange of skin on skin. Nellie puts her earrings on the dresser top and decides that she doesn't believe in altruism but she believes in this exchange, something hidden here always of laughter and sobbing, the space between the two. Husha will think the same thing as Nellie wedges her foot against the bathmat so her grandfather doesn't slip, a gesture replicated, half-remembered from some dream or read in some book or smoked in some drug. And always only half. The wrinkled flesh demonstrates against the smoothing palm in the bedroom and the warm bathwater the necessary action: it yields.

Something else yields, too, when Husha leaves her grandfather and turns off the light and shuts the door and heads down the hallway to her room, where Nellie waits. Something yields that is a necessary yielding for this new world. Husha will not speak of touch, not yet. Not in a way that others recognize, nothing more than a buzzing, a sawing of limbs against wings, a parting of warmth, fruit ribbed and shiny against her lips. Her grandfather might call for her in the night, might think she is his mother, his daughter, might think he is small and scared of heading off to school, might think he is having the nightmare of being young again. Always this in the night. Husha might look down and see she's holding a telephone, a bitten chunk of peanut butter toast, or might see Nellie, with cicadas for eyes, or teeth, either way.

Housecleaning [1]

ARTHUR, AFTER HIS STROKE TWO YEARS AGO, is too weak to cook or clean or buy groceries. He's strong enough to dress himself, but it takes fifteen minutes. He can change the kitchen garbage, but he can't always carry the bag down to the bin in the cellar, where it awaits being brought to the nearby dump. He can pull food from the fridge and put it in the microwave and bring it over to the small table by the window, but he can rarely transport the food without accident from plate to mouth, bits of egg or pasta or rice, spoonfuls of soup or yogurt slopping down his chin and the front of his shirt.

When, three weeks after his stroke, he slipped off a kitchen chair at lunchtime and wasn't found under the table until the following afternoon, when a neighbor came calling with a care package, his daughter, Husha's mother, was notified. She didn't have time to drive up herself, but in three hours she had hired a personal support worker to care for him—an arrangement that ended with the onset of the pandemic. Now Husha has taken the support worker's place. She gives Arthur less attention, but she also takes less advantage, and Arthur finds himself grappling with an unwieldy sense of independence as he opens his own dresser drawers, turns on the bathtub faucet, walks slowly but unfalteringly down the hall.

He's still too weak and uncoordinated to prep dinner or get behind the wheel of a car. He's too weak really even to garden, which he still tries to do in the mornings before the cicadas set to screaming, his knees and fingers plunged into the earth as if to plant himself. The earth steadies his tremors. His hands shake so steadily now that he can barely write his own name and so he rarely does; he has set aside his journals, the last one half-finished with three full pages of indecipherable wobbling scribbles that shrink finally into blank lines. He tried typing on Husha's laptop but found it took too long: bending to see the letters appear on the screen, pigeon-pecking the keys. The words left his head before they left his fingertips. Now with nothing left to do, with the cleaning and cooking and grocery shopping left to Husha, he listens to the radio and pretends to watch TV and puts books on hold at the library, which Husha retrieves. He reads, a task he can still complete with help from the battery-powered text magnifier that Nellie found online and ordered to the post office in town. He rests it on his knee, the book beneath, and reads and reads and reads and reads and reads.

Sometimes he lifts his head, remembers he has a neck and that it aches, and in a croak of voice, he speaks. On this day, when he lifts his head, the house is dark and the air smells warm, like hummus, sunbaked wood, or bread. His legs are skinny in his pants, marked out in the V-shaped bend of the chair cushion. Husha is restless and making a batch of soup that will hopefully last them the week. She pulls her hair behind her ears and dislodges nutmeg from beneath her fingernail with the tip of her tongue.

She listens to him as she stirs the contents of the pot. Vegetables and broth bubbling.

Do you know what the word *cryptic* means? asks Arthur.

Husha shifts her weight from hip to hip. Pulls at her lip with her teeth. Hidden, she says, then reconsiders. Coded.

Cryptic, says her grandfather, means *mysterious* or *obscure* or *enigmatic*. But when speaking of animals it means *camouflaged*. It means that something is in front of you, within sight, but you can't see it. It's the term used when something blends with its environment—which, you're right, feels closer to *hidden* or *coded* than it does to *enigmatic*. *Enigmatic*: a word with a definition that lacks definition, the inability to define, interpret, or understand. *Cryptic*, in the sense of *camouflage*, isn't difficult to interpret, only difficult to see. Cryptic beings inhabit two positions simultaneously, the position of themselves, their interior environment, and the position of their surroundings, their exterior. They take the world onto their bodies, their very skin or skeleton, while at the same time putting themselves out into the world, becoming part of it.

And you, says Husha, are speaking very cryptically.

By which you mean that you don't understand my meaning, or that I'm inhabiting two positions simultaneously, existing within multiple meanings?

Husha pushes the spoon to the bottom of the soup pot and scrapes up the potatoes that have begun to cling. By which I mean that I'm tired, she says, and you should get to the point before I take you to bed.

Arthur scowls. The book slips and he claws at it to keep it in his lap. At the back of the house, from the bathroom where she has been showering, Nellie begins to sing, a muffled, cottony sound caught between the walls.

Husha sighs. She watches her grandfather recover his magnifier and book, which in his haste has flipped closed. In the dim living-room light, she can see that the book is titled *Insects of Canada*. It's a current favorite of his, one he's working through meticulously, laboriously, and has already renewed once from the library.

You're talking about cicadas, she says. *They get into everything*, she thinks.

Sure, he says, we can go that route. I'm talking about cicadas.

Husha raises her eyebrows. What other routes are—

Cicadas, he says, are cryptic. That's why you never see them in the trees. Think about it—this place is ringing with them—but have you ever seen one?

Only the shells, says Husha.

Exactly, says Arthur, only the shells. Only the shape of what they *used to be*. Like an echo, but in material form.

Husha regards her grandfather from across the room, having forgotten for a moment the soup she should be stirring. Very poetic, she says, but what's the point?

What's the point of what I'm trying to say, or what's the point of cicadas being so cryptic?

Either, she says. Both.

Ah, there it is, says her grandfather: Either, *both*. As for the cicadas, they need to be hidden because they continually reveal their location to predators. They sit there, invisible but making noise, giving themselves away in the hopes of finding a mate. And don't give me that look, he says, shaking his finger and making her wonder what expression had crept across her face. It's not some romantic hoopla. That's one of the few things I'm certain I am not trying to say. Cicadas search for their mates compulsively, instinctually. There's nothing romantic or sweet about it, because there's nothing decisive about it. Did you know cicadas will keep mating even as their own bodies break down?

There's something romantic in that, isn't there? She smirks. Procreating against all odds?

Not if they haven't consciously decided to do it, Arthur says. The act simply becomes torturous, a horror show.

I guess it depends what you mean by "bodies breaking down."

Right, says Arthur, I should clarify. There's a fungal spore, *Massospora cicadina*—he taps the cover of the heavy book in his lap—that infects periodical cicadas, the kind we have outside right now, the sporadic kind. A species, I might add, we're only lucky enough to have in July because of that cold spring. The soil needs to be a certain temperature for the nymphs to dig themselves out.

Lucky? mutters Husha, thinking about her routine of closing the windows in the late morning to block out the noise.

Yes, lucky, says Arthur. They only come out of the ground every seventeen years. They're a nuisance, sure, but miraculous—the earthly equivalent of celestial events. Like the moon pulling the tide or the timed occurrence of eclipses. Anyway, what was I—? Ah, okay, this spore, *Massospora cicadina.* It grows beneath the cicada's exoskeleton and destroys it from the inside out until it's more fungus than bug. But affected cicadas still try to mate—as their limbs fall off, as their bodies split in two.

You're right, says Husha, leaning with her fingers tented against the counter. It's unromantic. Sounds like something out of a nightmare.

As she says this, she hears the fuzzy, static sound of the shower snap off down the hallway and remembers her soup on the stove. She turns and grips the spoon, which has grown hot against the side of the pot. It nearly burns her hand, and she curses softly. Nellie emerges from the bathroom with a towel around her hair and calls out as she moves toward the bedroom that something smells *good*, something smells *inspired*, *delicious*, *unbelievable*. Husha laughs and is relieved to see she hasn't burnt the soup after all.

Arthur sighs, feeling tired all at once, knowing his moment of holding Husha's attention has passed. He speaks anyway as she stirs the soup.

When beaten to a paste and eaten, he says, his voice mingling with the warm liquids in Husha's sight line, cicadas are medicinal—they're traditionally used by the Chinese to treat fever and nightmares.

Husha nods. She begins to hum.

The lesson being, Arthur continues, folding his hands together on top of the book and smiling wanly to himself, that if cicadas are the stuff of nightmares, then the stuff of nightmares should be beaten down and—he coughs, something waxy sticking in this throat—consumed.

* * * *

ARTHUR READS about how periodical cicadas lay their eggs in trees and wooded plants. He reads about how those eggs hatch and the baby nymphs fall to the earth and crawl into the ground, latching to roots and making themselves a nest, a home. He reads about how they wait patiently, like how clouds in the sky heavy with rain wait for their own coalescence as storms. He reads about how in late spring after seventeen years the cicadas do their housecleaning, tunneling their shelled bodies out of the soil.

Housecleaning [2]

HUSHA FOUND THIS BOOK IN LATE SPRING. She found it unexpectedly, while cleaning out her mother's house in London, something she tried to convince herself would be meditative, satisfying, provide her with a sense of closure. It was an obligation, her duty: she promised herself she would never complain. Besides, besides, besides, there wasn't anyone left to complain to. The funeral was over, a short ceremony only five people were legally allowed to attend because of the pandemic; Nellie had stopped answering Husha's calls; and her grandfather was back in the hotel room, so exhausted he was unable to lift his head from the pillow, saying only—I want to go north. Get me out of this goddamn city. Let's *go*.

She wouldn't complain, not even to herself. Not to her dead mother, whose absence still rang like the aftershock of an explosion in her ears. It wasn't a full housecleaning—she would do that later when she decided to sell the place—but it would still be hard work to clear the fridge and cupboards where the food had surely rotted, scrub the washrooms, remove her mother's ID and any valuables she could find, save any plants still living, vacuum, mop, and turn off the water and air conditioning. All of this, she hoped, would take under three hours.

Her mother's home was also Husha's home, her childhood home, and Husha was heavy with memory as she unlocked the front door. The rooms on the first floor smelled musty and thick, like dust, dying plants, trapped sunlight. The carpets were flat and quiet on the hardwood. The furniture and objects in these spaces were orderly. The couch cushions were fluffed and poised, the kitchen clean, the books arranged alphabetically between bookends. None of this order necessarily suggested premeditation in her mother's actions, none of it necessarily suggested foreknowledge, an awareness that her daughter would be coming to clean her house after she was gone. No—Husha's mother was always meticulous, the spaces she inhabited specifically curated to reflect the state of mind she wished to experience.

But the process of tidying her home in the hopes of tidying her headspace rarely worked, Husha felt. Her mother was hardworking but pensive; determined, focused, and yet faltering, melancholic, overly reflective. As a child, Husha would come upon her staring vaguely out a window, picking at the skin under her nails. Occasionally, when stress was high at work (Husha's mother worked as a business consultant, a job she confessed to hating and which often kept her for long hours at the office; to Husha, her mother's work was complicated and indistinct, full of research and numbers and statistical predictions, lengthy emails and phone calls peppered with financial jargon and meeting after meeting after meeting), she would hear her mother mumbling, while making dinner in the kitchen or sweeping the front entryway or loading laundry into the machine, about going on a trip, going *away*. The prospect always excited Husha, who had never been on a trip besides visiting her grandfather's cottage up north. She was too young to understand what her mother really meant.

As she grew older, Husha learned what other people thought of her mother's personality, her moods. Adults peripheral to

Husha—neighbors; her friends' parents; an aunt and uncle from her father's side of the family whom she sometimes saw around the holidays until they moved back to the East Coast, relatives who gave her chocolates and hugged her for too long and asked her stagnant questions like *How is school?* or *Do you like your teachers?* or *What do you do in your free time?*—taught Husha that most people believed her mother's severity and introspection to be some kind of survival mechanism, a hardened shell required to uphold and protect the emotional stability and work ethic of a single mother whose husband died soon after their child was born.

Do you think she'll ever recover? Husha's aunt would whisper to anyone listening. She could try dating, at least.

How's your mother? her friends' parents would ask. We worry about her sometimes.

It must be difficult, the neighbors would say, pausing to chat with each other on the street while walking their dogs. Being alone like that.

Despite not having one memory of her father, Husha assumed life would have been easier for her mother if he had been around. But she also understood her mother's contemplative side to be disconnected from any life event or context. Her mother's mood was enduring, not situational—integral to and deep-set in her mother's personality. She certainly wasn't happy, but she wasn't miserable. In fact, Husha had heard her mother express the opinion, time and again, that happiness wasn't an emotion that people truly experienced. Joy was genuine but occurred sporadically. The belief in happiness as a sustained state of being, according to her mother, was immature or adolescent, much like believing in fairy tales or taking wedding vows to heart: the concept of happiness was media-fed, delusional, self-indulgent.

Was there premeditation in her mother's actions, in the taking of those too-many pills with water before bed? Husha felt that, narratively, her mother's actions should have been premeditated. If her mother were in a book, if she were a character, it would make sense—it would be sensible—that her personality traits, her occasional cloudy dislocation from reality combined with her need for control, her conviction, would result in an uncomplicated suicide. But her mother had used pills before (three times Husha had been called to the hospital) to deal strategically with difficult situations, to receive immediate medical intervention, transparent and clinical care, instead of subsisting for months on a psychiatric waitlist. Her mother rarely made mistakes, but this didn't mean she never did, and as a result Husha couldn't determine if her mother had wanted to die or not. Much worse, she couldn't decide which narrative she preferred.

Pulling the contents of the fridge into large black garbage bags and clearing the cupboards took even less time than Husha expected. She was wasteful, did not differentiate, threw out wilted lettuce and cans of beans, frozen pizzas and bruised mushrooms, a swampy plastic jug of milk, half a bag of white rice, eleven large eggs sitting round with patience in their carton, ice cream, crackers, boxes of macaroni and cheese, a Tupperware of leftover pasta salad, half a brick of butter, and three raw chicken breasts—the flaccid stink of sticky, pink flesh.

Husha was quick to clean the bathroom and floors. Economical. She kept only one orchid and one succulent, which she transported out to her car and nestled in the backseat footwell. The rest of the plants, dead or half-dead, went to the curb. Husha moved with surety, precision. She felt feverish and full, as if a hiccup waited beneath but would not break from the bottom of her throat. A volcanic tension and acidity were building in her torso because she would not pause, did not hesitate, blank in mind and sight, unthinking—unthinkable, this task her body was completing—she looked at but did not see the framed photographs on the wall beside the staircase; a half-finished mug of coffee on the living-room side table, crescent-stained with lipstick; her mother's maroon rain jacket hanging flat-limbed by the door.

The muscles behind her eyes began to ache. The thick skin on the ends of her fingertips was numb. She went upstairs.

Her mother's bedroom, which she did not did not did not did not want to enter, was quiet, its door open. Lilac-purple walls. Large, dark-framed window. Someone—a police officer?—had stripped the sheets and blankets from the bed. Husha slowed, the bones of her arms and legs becoming malleable, walking as if moving carefully through quicksand, deep molasses, dream.

She found this book unexpectedly, shoved in the inch of space between two windowpanes beside her mother's bed.

If she had thought about it beforehand, if she had expected this book, she would have expected to find it tucked under the bed instead of beside it, cloaked in dust; or up on a shelf in the closet between the carry-on suitcase and winter gloves, strung with cobwebs; or beneath a loose floorboard on which Husha might catch her toe. In realizing she expected the book to be hidden under and beneath and behind, she also realized how cliché her expectations were of her mother, how entrenched they were in standard representations of motherhood-with-mental-illness, how maddeningly overdone and overly sentimental. The Gothic came creeping up the back of her neck like a cold hand—every old book she had read and every scary movie she had watched as a kid—every basement staircase, every attic crawlspace, every window staring out like a milky eyeball into the street. Everything that had ever taught her that suicide meant she should be terrified, that her mother's soul was restless, sleepless, wandering, bleeding, sealed into the walls of Husha's childhood home.

And why always *her* childhood home? Why not her mother's? Or the many places her mother had lived since she herself was a child, since and before she had Husha? Surely her mother's soul—if a soul was something Husha wanted to believe in—existed beyond the temporal location of her body's dying, beyond the space in which she had been a mother. Surely she existed beyond her daughter's *then*, the perceived sacredness of childhood, and her daughter's *now*, scrubbing floors, removing plants, cleaning up her mother's life. Surely her mother existed, even in death, beyond the confines of her daughter's mind.

What terrible, bland, and ungracious cliché it was to be shocked by her mother's probable suicide. What tasteless convention to expect that she should be surprised by her mother's death, that suicide, or at least an accidental overdose, should be unexpected. Husha wasn't so naïve. She had watched the movies, after all, and read the books, and witnessed the women go crazy—the ones who saw shapes in wallpaper or drove their cars into trees or put their heads into ovens (carefully, with damp cloths under the children's bedroom doors) or put stones in their pockets and walked into the river, the pond, the sea.

Husha wasn't so innocent as to think it only fiction.

But now there was her mother's book, this book, a fiction she had never expected. This unexpected bound volume, small, slight, with printed pages neatly aligned. And even worse and more degrading was the expectation hardly admitted to herself that here in this book would be hidden some note or final remark, like she was owed anything, any written mention of regret, which would also be a mention of love, like she required or deserved any further explanation.

Now there was this book, which Husha found wedged between the windowpanes. She wouldn't have found it at all if she hadn't pulled back the curtain beside the bed and looked down into the street as she knew her mother liked to do. It was the reason the bed was pushed so close to the window, snug up against the wall, so her mother, in the night when she couldn't sleep—sometime around three in the morning, what her mother called the Witching Hour, an insomniac time she also claimed had more to do with menopause than evil forces, although traditionally those were maybe one and the same—would sit up and pull back the curtain and look down on the street. Sometimes as a child Husha would come visit her mother after a nightmare, herself like a ghost in her pale pajamas, creaking open the door, the hallway silent and opaque behind her, and there her mother would be, already awake and looking out the window. Husha would experience one of those strange and disorienting moments of realizing her mother lived a life outside of the care she gave her daughter, realizing her mother might sit there, awake and in consciousness while she herself slept. Eventually, with age, that realization would transform into awareness, perception, acknowledgment, empathy. But first there was fear in the realization of object permanence, that her mother might sit up every night in the dark with those shadowed eyes, tented knees beneath the blankets.

What nightmare woke her? Husha would wonder, who had herself woken from nightmare. What nightmare could scare her, her mother?

On those nights, Husha would get into the bed and into the warmth surrounding her mother's body, and together they would look out the window and out at the city and her mother would say, It's an ocean out there and all the boats are coming in to shore. The streetlights would bob in Husha's tired eyes until she closed them and crossed the same ocean into slumber.

Now the street was stark and well lit, bald and as sore-looking as a waxed scalp. The sidewalks were clean and bare, and the grass was unbrowning itself after winter snow. Husha suddenly registered that it was springtime, that buds were swelling on the ends of tree branches like green-colored finger-nails, that squirrels were pulling up chunks of earth in search of long-buried nuts, that there was no more slush in the gutters. She registered, looking out the window, that it was springtime, and also registered that something had changed for her here, that springtime was no longer synonymous with rejuvenation, fresh starts. It was more like being woken suddenly from a deep sleep by the lights in the room turning on. She felt the need to turn away from the window and cover her eyes.

She felt exhaustion—an exhaustive lurch toward consistent breathing, continued living, that took the place of spring. She felt that exhaustive lurch inside her body, close to the heave of her gag reflex, as she went to let the curtain drop and saw the book wedged between two windowpanes. She pulled the first slab of glass aside. The dark, woven book cover was cold against her palms and fingertips as she pulled it free. She didn't mean to, but she broke the spine upon opening it, the sensation ricocheting up through her fingers like cracked knuckles.

Inside, a couple of pages deep, she found the table of contents:

Contents

She sat down on the sheetless bed and began to read.

[Unnamed]

HUSHA'S GRANDFATHER'S HOUSE, which is also the real and physical space that houses this book, is located off Curry Road in Fort Irwin, not far from Eagle Lake and, a little farther, the town of Haliburton. Unlike most houses on Curry Road, which are second homes, expansive cottages, for their Toronto-based inhabitants, and which face out toward the long, snaking stretch of Haliburton Lake, Arthur's house is on the opposite side of the road, within walking distance of what Arthur calls "the lake" but what could really be called a large pond, an unnamed circular stamp of water in the forest, like a blue thumbprint on a bird's-eye-view map.

Also unlike those other cottages, Arthur's home is small and ramshackle, asymmetrical, built haphazardly over many years. It started as a two-room cabin with a detached outhouse that he bought when he was young, wanting a place to escape his professorial duties during the summer months. Later, when he met Husha's grandmother and felt embarrassed by the humble getaway, he installed proper electricity and plumbing, turned the cabin into a combined kitchen and living room, and added a bathroom and bedroom that branched out from a hallway at the back. He didn't have a lot of money at the time and commissioned his brother-in-law, who worked in construction, to help him in return for three cases of beer and free babysitting whenever the need arose. The two men spent long summer days hauling two-by-fours out of the brother-in-law's truck bed, sweating through their shirts in the afternoon heat, chatting about the different properties of lumber—the one topic that functioned as an intersection between their professions—and hiding out under tarps that they had strung up in the trees when it started to rain. When Husha's mother came along, Arthur added another bedroom to the cabin and dug out a small cellar beneath the kitchen. By himself, he built the front porch and repaired the original cabin's sinking roof.

Inside, the ceilings are at different heights and the wall corners occasionally meet at odd angles. Some are drywall, others wood, and the windows are wide and plentiful. The living room and kitchen are separated only in an ideological sense by a stretch of kitchen counter attached to the wall by the back door and the transition from hardwood to tile on the floor. The couches in the living room are mismatched—one is faux leather and the other is covered in a gray, scratchy fabric. Arthur's lumpy chair with its deep cushion and big, curving armrests sits a little off to the side, facing in such a direction that he can see the inside of the stone fireplace, the forest outside the glass back door, and a theoretical person (a person who used to be his wife or daughter or support worker and is now his granddaughter) cooking with her back turned in the kitchen, all with minimal swiveling of his head. The rug on the living-room floor is Persian, patterned, and expansive, touching the feet of every piece of furniture in the room. The walls in the living room are painted maroon, in the kitchen, a soft cream, lighter than beige. Copper pots hang above the stove. Half-dead flowers are propped indefinitely in a vase on the counter, their petals wilted and faces bowed resolutely. The refrigerator is covered with to-do lists and takeout menus and old photographs—Husha as a child by the lake, her hair soaked and hanging in ringlets over her face; Husha's mother wearing overalls on top of a red string bikini; an overweight beagle with a stick in his mouth; Arthur and his wife, Sonia, with their arms around each other, squinting into the sun, mouths open as if caught mid-conversation, standing on the front porch.

Arthur has always loved the cabin and regarded it with a kind of reverence, but his wife frequently grew frustrated with his unrealistic plans to take down walls, add more rooms—perhaps a spiral staircase that led up into the trees. He was half-joking, but always hopeful about the project. He made sloppy architectural sketches on scraps of paper and taped them up to the hallway wall.

Three months before she died, Husha's grandmother was lying in a hospital bed and, from her position propped up with the rough hospital blanket tucked around her abdomen, begged Arthur to sell the summer home, the cabin. Pneumonia was filling her lungs and something funny was happening with her legs—they were swollen, she had trouble walking. Arthur had brought her her knitting to keep her company while he wasn't around, and she ran the pads of her fingers along the smooth wooden needles, which she held in her hands. Two balls of yarn lay—to Sonia, tangled; to Arthur, intertwined—in her lap. Call Catherine, she said. Please. Catherine was their real estate agent and longtime friend. Sonia must have known or at least suspected that after she was gone, Arthur would indulge in his reclusive tendencies, that he would keep to himself, to his books and his plants. That he would clam up, go north to that goddamn cabin, try to build a bunkie in the forest, maybe kill himself by falling from a ladder as he attempted, one by one and entirely on his own, to nail multicolored shingles to its roof.

Don't be stupid, said Sonia. She looked at him sternly, her
eyelids hiked up into their sockets. And don't be stubborn. I
know even after I'm gone you'll want to be stubborn against
me. To rebel against me. (She thought about but didn't mention how angry she knew he would be, after she was gone.)
For once in your life, she said, placing her thumbs against the
pointed ends of the knitting needles, could you just do what's
good for you and not necessarily what you want to do? For once
could you—

Sonia, Arthur said from his seat beside the bed, it's okay.
You don't have to worry. You won't have to worry.

No, she said. No, listen. She moved her hips like she wanted
to wriggle out from beneath the blanket and stand. Arthur
shook his head and placed a hand on her knee. She exhaled
roughly, as if her throat were made of sandpaper. I know I
won't be able to worry even if I want to, she said. But listen.
That house is falling apart. You don't—

At this point Sonia began to cough, a sharp hack that
slammed up from the bottom of her lungs to the roof of her
mouth, and she couldn't speak anymore. Arthur stood up to
find her a tissue to spit into. He rolled back the blanket and
massaged her feet and eventually she recovered her breath and
her voice, but she couldn't remember what she had wanted to
say, how she had wanted to say it. She figured he had understood, and she was right, he had. She fell asleep with her husband's hands wrapped around her toes, evening light falling
orange through the window. Arthur moved her knitting aside,
gathered his things, and left for the night.

Two days after his wife's funeral, Arthur called Catherine,
the real estate agent, and told her that he wanted to put his

house in London up for sale. Four months later, mid-October, he had moved permanently into the cabin up north.

* * * *

THE HOUSE is deep-set in the trees, far away and invisible from Curry Road. The driveway leading to the house is long and winding, rolling with soft ups and downs, marked here and there with the dirt scoop of potholes, and framed on either side with maple and pine like walls. The underbrush is thick, full of wildflowers and the green, anxious stubs of saplings. The air is clear and windless, smelling of moss—murky wood growth; damp, turned earth; the settled dust on the silty driveway; the baking flavor of the sun against leaves. Occasionally the soft triangles of a doe's ears shift between the trunks of trees. At night, there are deeper sounds, a lack of birdsong, distant frog croaks like elongated burps pushing up from the lake. Coyote yips flipping like somersaults over the hills. The soundless pressure of a wolf's paw displacing sand.

The driveway ends a distance from the house and overlooks the descent down to the lake. The lake is small, almost swampy, and has been shrinking for years. Arthur is sensitive to the expanding shoreline and the growing lake weeds, long like aquatic trees. He wonders if, when he dies and leaves the house to Husha, the lake will be gone, only a marsh remaining, mud and reeds and half-sunken logs, herons picking through murky spinning pools of trapped water after rainfall. Will the land be worth anything at all? He wonders about the ethics of inheritance—generational wealth in terms of land ownership— but can't see an alternative, wants the best for his family and descendants, if there are any, feels he's too old, exhausted, and out of touch to invent or refurbish a replacement system of societal structure. Besides, Husha will treat the lake well, will remember when there was water deep enough for swimming, when the sound of rain was slow and resonant on its welcome and alike surface.

From the driveway is a path leading up to the front porch. It's springy with woodchips and lined on either side with round stones of differing sizes. The porch at the end of the path is worn but strong, long wooden planks scuffed from uncountable footsteps. The house stands up small and squat behind the porch: wood-paneled siding, dark-shingled roof, heavy charcoal-colored door. The air that fills the gap between the end of the driveway and the start of the front porch is now hazy, smudged with summer heat but visually penetrable compared to weeks previous when the cicadas first lifted from the earth. Husha and Arthur had not yet arrived, were busy preparing for and attending the funeral, and Nellie's decision to join them still hung ahead of her in the future. The empty, reflective house windows were the only witnesses to the crowded, almost opaque but moving cloud of insects hoisting themselves like frantic worry into the air. Their sound was less a song than a high-pitched moan, a whine that transcended into a wail.

Overbearing, intangible noise, the cicadas surrounded the house, unobserved, and climbed up into the trees.

* * * *

BY THE time Husha and Arthur arrived in mid-July, the cicada song was full and thick, swarming like sonic pressure on the outsides of the car windows. Husha parked the car in the driveway and got out to help her grandfather from the passenger seat. She was careful to keep her purse, slung over her shoulder, on the opposite side of her body from the arm she offered her grandfather. She didn't want him bumped by the sharp corners of a book buried deep beneath her wallet, hand sanitizer, Kleenex, and car keys.

Her Face Inside Out (Ears and Teeth, Collaged)

I HAD A DREAM, says Nellie, that I cut off your ears and your grandpa's ears with a paring knife—it was as easy as cutting the skin off a peach, as easy as cutting through warm butter—and I took your ears and I put them on the windowsill in the sunlight so they glowed red and veiny. The cartilage was soft, the lobes were downy, and I filled them with soil like little pots, filled them with this moist dirt that smelled like rain.

You could smell in your dream? asks Husha.

Nellie squints, pulling her eyebrows together. I could, she says. And I could feel the ridges of the veins beneath the skin of the ears. I could taste the soil when I brought my fingers to my mouth—metallic, like tin or blood. The ears were small and pink, packed with dirt—I thought of piglets in the mud—and I could taste the beans, their smooth and warm squish like miniature organs, that sprouted from the soil. Two ears sprouted beans, and the others sprouted flowers, tiny yellow buttercup flowers, and I could smell the sunny perfume of their petals.

Nellie pauses. She looks dreamy, her forehead soft and yet concerned, her bottom lip pulled up in the beginning of a pout.

You ate the beans, says Husha. Did you pluck the flowers?

It was peaceful, says Nellie, not horrible like it should have been. You didn't seem to mind, not having any ears. And your grandpa was sleeping.

What did you do with the flowers, after you plucked them?

I ate them, too. They tasted like how grass smells after it's been cut. What do you think it means?

* * * *

HUSHA SITS folding laundry on the living-room rug, her legs folded beneath her, her body just another layer of folded fabric, and her grandfather across the length of the coffee table sinks into his chair, half-dozing, sinking into the open book in his lap. Husha fishes out sock pairs from the basket beside her and pushes them together with her thumbs, insiding one sock around the other. She usually wouldn't be so brazen, doing this in front of her grandfather—he hates this habit, claims it ruins the elastic on the sock, and she supposes he's right, but she knows too many socks would go missing otherwise. She imagines the socks lying against each other quietly in their drawers, flat and innocent, orderly, and then wiggling off like snakes or centipedes in the night, slinking under the dresser or under the bed, in the crack between the bookshelf and the wall, into closet corners, beneath the rug.

Arthur already has a habit of misplacing his spare change (useless now, anyway, with all the stores putting up laminate signs banning cash), his box of collected stamps, and the silk ties he likes to pull out and touch on weekend evenings when Nellie gets takeout pizza from town. The pizza, propped with its box open on the coffee table in the living room, plates balanced on their laps, swamps the three of them in memories. The taste of the pizza—the salt and grease and tomato sauce—reminds them of public events, pre-pandemic. They grow thoughtful as they chew, reminiscent.

Nellie thinks of first-year residence parties, years ago now, the smell of spilled beer on the carpet, snow and silence outside the window three stories down, and music like a mallet on her

skull, the whirl of the multicolored Christmas lights she had
strung above her bed's headboard, mimicking her roommate,
trying to fit in, and some boy with dark fuzz on his upper lip,
narrow shoulders hugging her from behind, his hands sliding
across her stomach, lips slurring through her hair, *You're so
fucking gorgeous*, and Nellie wheeling around, out of his grip,
watching him lift his hands up and squeeze imaginary breasts
in the air (later that night, or near morning, the sky turning
hazy gray outside, he would beg her to come to bed with him,
on his knees in mock subjugation, hugging her thighs, and she
would relent, on her back on the spring mattress, orgasming
quickly, almost quicker than him, with this image of his face
looking up at her, wanting her badly enough to whimper, chin
tucked between her legs).

Husha thinks of movie nights with friends left over from
high school, the creamy butter smell of the Cineplex lobby,
large, animatronic figures flying their dragon-winged airplanes
overhead, arcade machines buzzing, kids with tickets in hand
squealing and rushing off down the hall, mothers trailing
with drink trays, surfaces sticky, workers stuffing exhaustion
back behind their eyes and down into their throats—*Hi there,
how can I help you? What can I get you? What can I do for
you?*—cup holders beside the cushioned seats slightly greasy,
and everything blinking, everything seeping colored lights and
sound, everything organized and orchestrated like a second-
rate Disneyland, an onslaught of sensory stimulation, a world
isolated from the everyday, the mundane, and therefore divert-
ing, fantastic, Husha's fingers tingling on the ends of her hands
as the movie bled into reality onscreen.

Arthur thinks of the bar three blocks down the street from

where he first lived with Sonia, his wife, that bungalow house in London, how the orange bar lights made her skin look dewy atop her cheekbones and around her chin, how she would place her elbow on the booth table between them and drop her hand onto his chest, how he would wear silk ties.

Husha usually wouldn't be so brazen, balling the socks up together in front of her grandfather, but he's sleepy and has put his glasses aside, and, anyway, he already has a habit of misplacing things—his spare change, his stamps, his silk ties. She insides the socks out, one around the other. Too many would go missing otherwise.

She's nearly finished with the basket, the clothes a neat stack beside her on the couch, when Nellie comes in with the groceries. Her hair is in a loose bun, hanging down by her neck. She's wearing baggy jeans and a striped T-shirt, a ring of sweat along her hairline and collarbone. She shuts the front door against the sound of the cicadas (always this sound, in the background of everything) and hauls the bags onto the kitchen counter.

Arthur startles awake, opening and closing his dry mouth, eyeing the pile of clothes on the couch, perhaps to see what Husha has done with the socks, perhaps as a measure of how much time has passed. In the kitchen, the faucet rushes open, cool water that Nellie splashes up onto her face. She washes her hands.

So, I was thinking, says Nellie, above the sound of the water hitting the sink.

Husha resumes folding. Were you? she asks.

While grocery shopping, Nellie continues.

Mm-hm, murmurs Husha.

About baby teeth, says Nellie. Or, more specifically, the skulls of children.

41

Husha looks up, one lifted eyebrow puckering the skin of her forehead, her expression leaning into a smile. On the other side of the coffee table, Arthur has leaned back in his chair. A small noise like sighing escapes his mouth.

Husha echoes him: she exhales. Explain, she says.

Have you ever seen a picture of a kid's skull? Nellie snaps the faucet off and dries her hands on a tea towel hanging by the stove. It's demented, she says. Here, let me show you.

She moves around the kitchen counter, pulling her phone out of her pocket. She leans over the back of the couch and passes the bright screen to Husha, who has lifted herself up onto her knees to reach over the folded pile of clothes. Husha's fingertips, as she takes the phone, slip across the inside of Nellie's wrist.

Did you get ice cream? asks Husha, thinking of the bags of groceries on the counter. It's a rhetorical question and they both know it—Nellie always gets ice cream when she goes to town. It's summer, after all, the thick soupy middle of it, and nothing tastes better on a metal spoon in front of an open window, the sun coming in through the screen.

Focus, says Nellie, pointing to the phone.

It'll melt, says Husha.

It'll refreeze, says Nellie, but she turns and goes back to the kitchen, pulling her hair out of its knot as she moves, tying it back up at the top of her head. She sets her hips against the counter ledge, begins to open and pick through the bags.

Raspberries and green onions and granola and pasta. Oreo ice cream and salmon and garlic, avocados, cans of black beans and chickpeas. Arugula. Quinoa. Eggs. Husha looks down at the phone in her hand and thinks of dinner—what will she make for dinner? Maybe she can pass the task off to Nellie tonight. She's tired already, and it's only two in the afternoon. She hasn't been sleeping well, she's been dreaming, something about opening the windows and letting the rain come in onto the bed, the covers soaked and swaddling her, she wakes sweating. Yes—she's been dreaming often of rain.

So? says Nellie, bending to put a container of yogurt on a low shelf in the fridge.

Husha refocuses her mind on the screen in her hand. *Refreezes her mind*, she corrects herself, her brain like a tub of melting Oreo ice cream—in this heat, perhaps there is no difference.

She grimaces. The image on the screen is a clean, slightly yellowed human skull, like one that might belong in a science museum or a high school biology textbook. The eye sockets and nose are empty and cavernous, spilling shadows. The chin is narrow. The cheekbones look underdeveloped, but Husha can't see much of them. Above and below the rows of squat children's teeth comprising the mouth are two rows of longer, rectangular adult teeth. Four rows in total, what seem layers and layers of teeth, a clustered, crowded, bone-filled face, reaching up almost to the eyes. Husha pauses with the phone in her hand. To think that all children look this way, beneath the skin. To think, Husha ponders, that we all used to look this way, our futures crouched invisible and waiting in our own bodies, as unrelenting as molars locked in bone.

Nellie's arm appears over her shoulder, snagging the phone.

So, she asks, what do you think?

What do *you* think? says Husha. You're the one who brought it up.

Nellie tilts her head. Her hair falls a little out of its bun. I think it's a shame all of the teeth have to grow in, she says.

Husha scoffs, though her thoughts had been wandering close to the same sentiment. A bit melodramatic, she says. Have you made it into a metaphor?

I'm serious! says Nellie. I think it would be healthy to have something waiting inside of us, something physiological, musculoskeletal—to not have our bodies entirely finished or solved. It would guarantee psychological growth, too, wouldn't it? If there were some new and inevitable experience waiting for us, inside of us?

You're just scared of dying, says Husha. Of growing old.

Now who's being melodramatic? asks Nellie. She waves a hand at Husha, brushing her words out of the air with her fingertips as if Husha's comments are inconsequential, obvious. She continues: Anyways, besides all that—

Besides dying?

Yes, besides dying.

Is there anything besides dying?

Come on, says Nellie, you really want to do this right now? It's two in the afternoon.

You showed me a picture of a child's skull.

It wasn't essential that the child be dead. That wasn't the point. I wanted you to see the design—

If you wanted me to see the design, you could have shown me an X-ray. It *is* essential that the child be dead.

Nellie stares at her, her body still bent and leaning over the couch. Arthur shifts in his chair, his breath hauling up out of his chest in a long sigh. It's unclear whether he's asleep, whether he's been listening. Surely they must have woken him. Husha closes her eyes and tries to relax the muscles in her jaw. She folds her hands in her lap.

The afternoon light coming in through the window looks soft on Husha's hair. Nellie pauses for a moment, listening for the background murmur of the cicadas outside—there in the background, always, the white noise of the cicadas singing. She wants to roll her abdomen forward against the lip of the couch and cup Husha's chin in her hands. She wants to draw her hands back along Husha's jawline and move aside her hair and put her thumbs against the freckles on her neck. She wants to say, I didn't mean anything by it. But she will not argue for innocence, not by claiming good intentions. She knows by now that there is more to love than good intentions.

Instead she squeezes the couch, like squeezing the words from her mouth, and says, I'll make dinner tonight. She backs away and goes to the kitchen, finding a place for the raspberries in the refrigerator, sliding the cereal into the cupboard. The baseboards, she notices, need dusting. And there is a smudge of fingerprints on the kitchen window. She reaches for a cloth. Something in her is still growing, although it at first resembles the opposite: an ability to pull back, pull away—she imagines this *something* like fingernails retracting into the skin, something inside her refusing to claw and scratch, irritate. This something *is* growth, she reflects, in that it rejects destruction, the combative draw of self-assertion. What can be left in this gap but growth? What can occur in this receding, this releasing, but cultivation?

Incubation, she answers herself. She thinks of the periodical cicadas, quiet before this summer, sleeping underground.

Husha unlaces her fingers, spreading them across her knees. She listens to Nellie moving behind her in the kitchen. *Is there anything besides dying?* It was unwarranted aggression on her part, certainly, but it's an idea that's been bothering her, sitting solid like immobility inside her limbs. It's an idea that grows like fungal spores in her mind. It's the root of the grace she sees in her grandfather's body (she studies him there, dozing on the other side of the coffee table). It's the root of the wonder Nellie sees in the child's skull. Is there anything besides dying? It isn't fully a rhetorical question—she really wants to know. Does dying not plunge its fingers and teeth into everything? Every individual moment that, like a scene in a movie, she pauses to inspect and decides she wants to remember? And if dying isn't in the moment itself, then the moment is a tribute to dying. A recognition and celebration of dying. All of this labor and dedication to each other, all of this work that goes into daily living, is no more than an acceptance of and appreciation for the process of dying. I will care for you, she thinks, looking at her grandfather's slumbering body, listening to Nellie put away the rest of the groceries, as you are dying. I will labor in respect of this life that is going. I will work now to honor the leaving.

Husha stands and neatly places the folded laundry in the basket. She joins Nellie in the kitchen and lifts herself on tiptoe to place her mouth against Nellie's earlobe. It's a voiceless moment. Nellie shivers and wraps a hand around Husha's hip.

* * * *

NELLIE'S FULL name is Eleanor, a name that came from her mother's sister, her aunt, who passed away just before Nellie was born. It was a sentimental decision, her naming. Nellie's mother was understandably dissatisfied with the way her sister had died and wanted to round off her story, edit the ending. Her sister, Nellie's aunt, had been in a terrible and sudden car accident. The accident had in no way been her fault, neither was it something she could have prevented. Nellie's mother would not provide details, but once Nellie got her uncle alone while he was drinking during a family gathering and questioned him about the incident.

She was a careful woman, he said. Always very worried.

Who? asked Nellie. Aunt Eleanor?

Her uncle nodded. She was the kind of woman who checked the flight history of her plane's pilot before traveling, who checked that the front door was locked—twice—before going to bed. As a kid she made us all do fire drills, made us throw rope ladders out of windows and test metal doorknobs with the backs of our hands. She was neurotic, annoying. We loved her a lot.

And the car accident? asked Nellie.

Her uncle sighed. She was going down the 401 in the middle lane. Middle of the day, great weather. A truck in the right-hand lane lost control and accelerated and barreled her into the median in the center of the highway. The police claim she died instantaneously. Which I guess is probably true.

But what happened? Was there anything else? Mom won't talk about it, won't say a word.

Her uncle coughed quietly and took another drink from his beer. He looked past Nellie at the rest of the family mulling about the kitchen. I guess there was some difficulty identifying the body, he said. El was—ah, how to put it nicely—decapitated by the truck. I guess—I guess it happens more often than you'd think.

At that moment Nellie's grandmother, who was a small, waddling woman with sloping shoulders and curly white hair, walked into the room and saw their faces and said, What're you talking about?

Eleanor, said her uncle.

Ah, said her grandma. Eleanor. She was a careful woman, very intense.

Mm, said her uncle.

Her grandmother lowered herself onto the couch, stared at the TV for a moment, which was silently playing a football game, subtitles on, and said, Thinking of Eleanor feels like a toothache, a kind of throbbing. Other times, thinking of her feels like a bruise at the top of my nose, in my head. She pointed to the space between her eyebrows. Other times it feels like that tug in your throat before swallowing, like the need to cough. Sometimes I forget that she's gone and think that I should pick up the phone because we haven't spoken in a while. Why hasn't she called me? Has she forgotten my number, where I live? Has something happened to her, is anything wrong?

Sometimes, said Nellie's grandmother, I forget about her entirely. In my mind I only ever had two children. The forgetting isn't bad, either—it's a blankness, simple, certain. It's so easy, like falling asleep. She glanced at Nellie, shrugged, dragged the back of her hand against her mouth. A bit of relief.

After that evening and that conversation with her uncle and grandmother, Nellie refused to be called Eleanor or El. Nellie was bad enough but would have to do. The name was papery in her mouth, old and as if coated with dust.

Indecision

HUSHA STANDS IN THE BEDROOM she shares with Nellie and holds her mother's book in both hands, testing its weight. Solid, material. Irrefutable reality, and yet the contents, she thinks, are fiction: a meandering narrative, stories. She hasn't read all of the book yet, not even half. After about fifty pages, and before the start of the first short story, she found herself unable to progress.

Is the book even supposed to be read linearly? she wonders. Is progression even something she should expect?

Is the book even supposed to be read—? This is the question that makes her, each time she opens the book, close it and put it away. Did her mother want her to read the book? Should it be in her possession? It all depends on her mother's intentions, whether she meant or didn't mean to die. Then Husha thinks, whether her mother meant or didn't mean it, it happened, and by her own hand. Her own fault, regardless. The same disaster, regardless of who drops the bomb or their intentions behind the explosion. Husha's anger, disapproval, disgust, rolls up shaking into her wrists.

She looks out the bedroom window and sees the sun plunging down into the treetops. She drags her fingertips across the rough book cover and steps out into the hall.

The shape of her grandfather's body is small and tilted ahead of her. He's also moving down the hall toward the kitchen, having just come out of the bathroom. His hands are damp from washing, and he pulls them along the length of his forearms to cool his skin. He loves this house, but it isn't air conditioned. He's overheated nearly every summer day. Each fall arrives like palpable relief in his body, like airways opening after long compression—damp, furtive discovery of residual energy. He imagines taking deep breaths down by the lake, the wind against his face, dirt cool on the bottoms of his feet because he has taken off his shoes—

He smiles softly with anticipation, still excited for the changing of the seasons, the turn of the earth, time moving on with or without him, as he walks down the hall, back bent, into the tight, evening grasp of summer heat.

Husha watches him slouch along, rubbing his forearms with his hands. The house is quiet besides the sound of his feet sliding against the hardwood: the lowering sun lulls the cicadas to sleep and Nellie—by far the loudest of the three—has gone out for a walk, snagging rare private time before the mosquitoes sift out from the long grass between the trees.

Grandpa, says Husha as her grandfather enters the kitchen and steadies himself against the counter. She notices a cluster of dishes in the sink that Nellie has neglected to wash. She notices the dried, smudgy prints of someone's dirty foot on the tile floor. She socks these details away in the back of her mind, a mental checklist to complete later, and touches her grandfather's elbow, guiding him to his chair.

Yes? he says. You startled me. But he appears sedate, calm.

Mm, she murmurs, acknowledging his surprise. Sorry. I have something to show you.

They settle into the living room. Husha snaps the lamp on, chasing the shadows off her face. Do you recognize this? she asks, placing the book against her kneecaps.

Arthur squints. A new library book? he says, reaching out a hand.

Husha shakes her head. She passes him the book. He rotates his torso toward the side table, retrieving and sliding his glasses onto his nose and the magnifying book reader into his lap.

It's heavy, he says absently, regarding the thick cover and pages.

As a boulder, she says, and attempts but fails to laugh.

He opens the cover and leans closer to study the first page.

At this moment the front doorknob turns and Nellie comes in from her walk, a slight sweat dancing with the distant lamp-light on her forehead and her hair down and in a mess against her neck and cheeks. Husha wants to say, *Shush*, as Nellie makes a racket closing the door and kicking off her shoes and spinning—yes, she spins—into the front foyer. Husha stops herself from speaking, doesn't quiet Nellie or ask her to slow, because in this moment Nellie is so beautiful, her collarbones like shelves holding shadows, a damp, heated wind following her through the door, and a wide purpose in her eyes, vacant wonderment, as she catches Husha's gaze across the room.

You should see the lake right now, she says, breathless. It's orange with the sunset. And the cicadas have shut the hell up for once and let the rest of the forest have a chance. The cicadas feel like they press downward, don't they? Like putty in your ears. Have you ever heard bullfrogs call to each other across the water? They're horrible and musical all at once. She laughs. And the stars are poking out above the trees. And the loons—but they must be on the other lake. And the—oh, shoot, sorry, she says, having reached the back of the couch, putting her hands in Husha's hair. She looks at Arthur with the book in his lap. Am I interrupting something? she asks. Group story time?

Husha smiles weakly. Arthur looks up, a knot forming between his eyebrows.

A pause descends. Arthur purses his lips. It isn't the worst idea, he says.

Husha laces her fingers together. Did she tell you about this? she asks.

Did who tell you about what? asks Nellie.

I knew she was writing something, says Arthur. I didn't know it was this.

That's your mother's? Nellie tosses her head, gesturing toward the open pages in Arthur's lap. Your mother wrote a book?

It's more like a collection, says Husha.

So you've read it? asks her grandfather.

No, she says. She corrects herself: Not much.

It's not a sin to have read it, he says.

I don't know if she left it for me.

His forehead softens. His eyes are lost behind a glint of lamp-light reflecting off his glasses. Does it matter? he asks.

Nellie grinds her thumbs into Husha's shoulders excitedly. No, it doesn't, she says. We're reading it. Tonight, preferably.

Nellie, stop it, says Husha, shaking off her grip.

What?

You know what.

I don't, actually.

Enough, Husha says. She stands up from the couch. Forget it. She grabs the book from her grandfather's lap, nearly knocking the magnifying reader off his knee. Snapping the cover shut, she swings around the couch and heads back down the hallway.

This house isn't that big, calls Nellie, feeling that to not push the matter further would be an admission of guilt, of ill intent. She's still elated, can still smell the evening air in her clothing. There aren't that many hiding spots, she says.

Don't test me, barks Husha, barely audible down the hall. The bedroom door claps like an echo behind her.

* * * *

DESPITE HUSHA'S apparent decisiveness, the book—this book—appears two days later, on the mantel above the fireplace. Nellie is tempted to personify, feels it watching them.

No one mentions the book. Certainly, no one reads it.

Laundry Day

THIS IS WHAT IT'S LIKE:

This is how it feels:

Husha is walking down the hallway, carrying a basket of laundry. The hallway is long, stretching the length from the laundry room to the bedrooms to the washroom and ending in the kitchen. The basket of laundry is full, clothing heaped and layered nearly past her head, teetering. She hoists it onto her hip. It's been a long day. The last thing she must do on this long day is bring the laundry down the hall in its basket and place it on the floor in the living room and fold it (the laundry room itself is too small for this chore). After this she can sleep.

Somewhere back between her ears is an ache she can't remember developing. It's the memory of pain, like the recollection of a dream that occurred during anesthesia, during distant incision, surgery. Blunt, numb, blurred aching. She ignores it.

As she walks with the basket on her hip, a sock dislodges from the pile and floats to the floor. It's a small sock, blue-and-white striped. As she kneels to pick it up, her fingertips sweeping the floor, a bra tumbles, and then another sock. She tucks the first sock back into the pile and then bends to snag the bra and second sock, and, as she does so, successfully scooping them onto separate fingers, a pair of underwear falls, and then a pair of shorts. Husha comprehends the futile pattern and places the basket on the floor, taking her time with the shorts, folding them before putting them back to ensure they won't fall again. Then she stands and starts down the hallway.

54

She doesn't make it very far. Again this ache back between her ears, just above the base of her skull, a shadow of sensation, upsets her rhythm. A sock falls, she bends to pick it up, another tumbles, she comprehends the pattern—comprehends it but cannot alter it. There is some necessary adjustment she can't see, blurred by this ache in her head, some change that she can't accomplish because she can't unveil what it could possibly be. Slowly she crouches and piles the laundry again, slowly she moves down the hallway. But if she moves, she moves backward, this must be the case, must be for certain, because the hallway stretches farther now than it did before. To her left is still the laundry room, the washing machine waiting with its sideways jaw hanging open. What dirt has already accumulated in the fabric in her arms? What freshness fades in the clothing she must fold and put away? Beneath her eyes, beneath her nose, exists a low blankness—a plane of nothing like darkened glass. Has she misplaced something—somebody? Has a blue-and-white striped sock skittered away? Her personal Sisyphus is a slipping of the mind back down the laundry mountain. She looks down the hallway. She looks down at the pile of laundry in the basket. She will bend and pull up the loose clothing, again, again.

This is what her mother's death is like, two months after the happening and the knowing deep—deep—and the settling. This is how living and working and forgetting feels.

Grief: Can this be a word to describe the mundane? Husha finds it at once impossibly lofty, unbearably cheap.

The Dreaming, in the Gloaming

I'VE HAD THE STRANGEST DREAM, says Arthur.

He's sitting up in bed with blankets pouched around his waist. The skin on his chest, what is visible beneath his loose tank top, is soft and lumpy and ribbed—in the darkness, the skin slides with the eye as one into the blankets and sheets and pillows. He appears to be emerging from the bed like surfacing from inside a swamp, pulling his limbs from the muck of nightmare.

Husha sits on the edge of the mattress. She heard him yelling and came slouching half-asleep into his room, like ocean water smearing onto shore.

Do you think dreams can hang around? Arthur asks. Do you think they can stick to walls? He pauses for a moment, running his hands along the bedspread. Husha feels that he's watching her, though she can't see where his eyes are pointed, whether they are open or closed. She closes her eyes slowly to a deeper darkness, and then opens them again to the shape of her grandfather's body silhouetted against the gray wall. She can faintly see the wispy hair on his head sticking straight up, can faintly see, outside, the pine trees turning sepia-toned in the coming daylight. She hears a clock ticking somewhere high up on a wall, always in this old house a clock ticks somewhere.

Here, in her grandfather panting on the bed, is an urgency that doesn't fit with the feeling of infinity in the house.

Do you think, he says, not waiting for her to answer his first questions, dreams are just recycled memories? Scrapbooked memories, collaged? Do you think they can be trapped places like trapped air, or in objects, like pressing a flower between the pages of a book? Do you think what I touch with my mind is the same as what I touch with my hands, that there is some similar influence on the world around me? Do I make an impression? And if a thought can touch, then a dream—a real dream, you know the kind—is like a punch with a fist. Like a fist on drywall, for example, or a fist on glass, but nothing breaks, only absorbs.

Do you think you can have a dream, he says, and not remember the dreaming?

Do you think some leftover dream could have snuck inside my head?

Husha sits quietly. She's deciding whether or not to reach out and touch him, whether or not to ask whose dream he thinks he dreamt, when she hears a hitch in his throat and realizes Arthur is crying. She hears blurred hiccups, the smack of the heel of his hand against his wet cheek. The ragged intake of breath.

She was standing there in the hallway, he says. So easily. As if it was nothing. As if nothing had happened.

He shakes his head roughly like trying to shake water from his ears.

But it was me standing there, he says. And it was so easy to be standing there as her, and to look down at my hands, and to see myself in the mirror when I looked up. It was so easy to breathe as her, as if nothing had happened.

He must still be half-asleep, thinks Husha, watching the outline of his shoulders buck up and down.

It was me, he says, sobbing. It was me, it was me, it was me.

* * * *

THE NEXT DAY, as Husha passes the mirror in the hallway, she stops and looks at herself until she is unrecognizable, looks at her hair until it isn't her hair, her eyes until they aren't looking back at her. Like listening to a song until you hate the music. Like repeating a word until it becomes strange and tasteless on your tongue.

* * * *

THE LAST time Husha saw her mother was in February of that year. Her mother had cut her hair short so it hung in a blunt, choppy line at the same height as her earlobes. She was economical: once a year—usually in the summer—she went to the hairdresser and told them to cut it off, cut it all off, and then she paid them sixty dollars plus tip and left within thirty-five minutes of sitting down. Husha was in the final semester of her master's program at the University of Toronto and had driven to London to stay for a night. She wanted to see some high school friends who still lived in the city and also pick up a T4 slip that had arrived at her mother's address in preparation for the upcoming tax season. Her mother offered for Husha to stay at her place—You'll always have a room here, she said—but Husha responded, No, that's okay, I'll be out with Julianne in the evening so I might as well stay with her.

I'll take you up on that offer next month, though, she added. For the party. Husha's mother was turning fifty-six at the end of March and had uncharacteristically planned herself a birthday party. At this point in time, in February, Husha was still uncertain who had been invited, who would show. Of course, with the pandemic tumbling its way across the world, she would never find out.

At the house, when Husha arrived to retrieve her tax form, her mother was busy wiping the dining-room baseboards with a damp cloth. It was Saturday morning and Husha was hungover after spending the night out with her friend Julianne. She would drive directly back to Toronto after grabbing the form, make it to her apartment in time for an afternoon nap and a couple of hours in the early evening to work on a seminar presentation that was due the following week. As her physical body stood in her mother's entryway, her brain was elsewhere, her thoughts already nestling into the tomb of books she would retrieve from her bookshelf in Toronto and tracing the precise length of her presentation's opening lines. Dully, backstage of the performance of sensation, she could feel her wrists and knuckles aching from the cold. Her mother looked up briefly from her chore as Husha knocked her winter boots together and scrubbed their rubber soles against the mat by the front door.

On the table there, said her mother, tipping her chin toward the brown envelope with Husha's name printed on the front.

Thanks, said Husha. She took the envelope into her hands. You cut your hair, she said.

Yeah, said her mother, the ends were frizzing on me. But now I can't find my clip, you know, the green one, and it's always hanging down around my face. She sat back on her heels and placed the damp cloth on one of her knees and reached up to tug at the ends of her hair, as if to make it longer, to pull it out of her head.

It won't take long, said Husha, to grow back.

Her mother shrugged. Half a year, she said. Maybe more. She took the cloth off her knee and squeezed it in her hands. How's school? she asked.

Busy, said Husha.

And Julianne?

Ah, the same. She's good.

Well, said her mother, turning back to the baseboards. Be careful on the icy roads.

* * * *

IN HALF-DREAMS sometimes she halfway wakes to her mother's house, calling for her through the hallways and up the stairs: Mom? Mom! Mom! White sheets cover all the furniture and are spread along the floor, hang across doorframes and billow out of closets. Husha tears at them with her fingernails, pulling them off and down and out. In her half-sleep, her eyes are half-closed and the house is blurry, becoming murkier as she walks through it, uncertain of itself. She trips and lands hard on her elbows, looks down to see that the sheets have tangled around her ankles. Looks down to see that her feet have detached themselves from her legs and begun to hop-walk away, that they trail the sheets from their Achilles' tendons like strange, cumbersome scarves.

And now Husha, feet-less, is dragging herself on her stomach up the stairs, always up the stairs, to where she hopes to place her hands, flat-palmed, against the texture of her mother's lilac walls. To place her cheek, the side of her face. She's tired, her head is so heavy. She can't see anything—she tugs at her eyelids but they won't come off.

* * * *

SHUSH, says Nellie, holding her. Shhh.

Husha feels that she will shriek soon, that something will bore out of her chest like a cicada tunneling out of dirt into sunlight. She cannot grasp the edges of the huge undoing that folds outward through her skin.

Shhh, says Nellie, rocking her back and forth in the bed. Shush now, shhh.

* * * *

IN TRADITIONAL Chinese medicine, says Arthur, cicadas are sacred. They're medicinal and can be beaten into a paste and eaten to cure night fever. Do you have night fever, my Husha?

Husha stands outside in the afternoon light that has just begun to touch the tops of trees. Somewhere nearby she can hear water moving, although she knows the lake is too far for her ears to catch the sound of waves lapping.

My Husha, have you been sleeping?

The sound, she realizes, is less like a lake and more like a river, more like a river running through her head.

My Husha, have you been dreaming?

More like a river running from ear to ear. She stands in the afternoon light and listens to the water, which is maybe more a deep humming, like cicadas singing low. She stands in the light and holds a cicada in her hands, on its back, upside down, legs waving slowly like rotating feelers. It fell onto her head, into her hair where it stuck and scrambled, as she walked.

Arthur looks up from his book, up at her. My Husha, have the night fevers given you dreams?

She feels the wings break first, crunching like a plastic bottle, as she pinches her fingers together. The legs stop waving and instead flinch, twist, bend sharply outward at incorrect angles as her fingers split its body apart. Beneath the exoskeleton is the soft, brainy flesh of the bug.

My Husha—

She expects warmth, but the innards are neutral in her hands. She feels the sun in her hair and along the side of her face. She begins to mash the dark goop, chunky with shell shards, between her fingers.

And these cicadas, in particular, says her grandfather, having stayed underground for seventeen years, incubating—

She kneads the mixture.

—resting—

Gets it beneath her nails.

—must surely house some greater medicine than their yearly siblings. Something older.

Gets it in the lines of her palms. Massages it.

Something heavier.

Her hands are heavy, sticky with the remnants of the cicada. Still the river, the cicadas singing, rushes through her ears. She brings her hands to her mouth.

And deeper. Deeper now she feels the pull of the cicada's innards against her tongue. A squeeze and a buckle now at the back of her throat.

Optional/Redacted/Wrapping Open Wounds

IN THE EVENING, WORDLESS, Husha brings the book down from the mantel. The three of them settle by the fireplace with the book between them, open, and the windows dark behind them.

Part Two

A Mirror
Walking
Down

The Surfacing

1

Mama, look, the little girl says, holding out her hand. Her fingers are dark red, as if bruised. On her palm is a raspberry, plump, pulled from the bush at the back of the yard—a sphere of thick lumps. She brings it to her mouth and whispers in its ear.

Mama, look.

* * * *

THE FISH, if it is a fish, lives somewhere in the waters between the west coast of British Columbia, the islands of Hawaii, and Japan. She glimpsed it once before in the submarine, sitting and watching, as is her custom, the live footage from the cameras coasting along the ocean floor, eleven thousand feet below her in the water. The screens in the observation room are arranged in a grid pattern, pixelated livestream set atop and beside pixelated livestream, like the simultaneously split and interconnected viewpoint of a fly.

Viewpoints, she corrects herself.

Looking at these screens, looking as if through the eyes of a fly or some other multi-eyed insect, she can see the ocean floor from every angle—or almost every angle. She can't see behind, although sometimes she can see the camera itself from behind, as another camera trails it for a moment, crossing its path. The ocean is always dark, but the lack of a backward-facing camera feels like a deeper darkness. For this reason she's exhausted after sitting for too long in the observation room. She's tackled—as she would describe it—by emptiness, numbness, the bluntness of invisible pain. Sitting here is like trying to locate a headache on the surface of the scalp when the injury is inside the brain.

Rolling, rolling: the ocean floor rolls smoothly by, illuminated briefly by the camera lights.

She once asked Anthony, the head of research, about this blind spot. Why can't we put a camera on both sides of the probe?

We can, he answered. He blinked at her, a little surprised, it seemed, that she would ask such a stupid question. *Less advanced.* She had worked with him for five years and knew this was the kind of vocabulary he used. Not *stupid* but *less advanced.* This language, he reasoned, was more encouraging. It suggested a possibility for improvement.

We can, he answered, but why would we? Each of those cameras costs more than you want to know, and what would be the use in seeing the ground we've already covered? Redundant, he said. Unnecessary.

Yes, what would be the use? She couldn't answer the question, at least not in those terms, in his terms, in terms of use. Maybe she can't answer the question at all. But she finds herself, every once in a while as she sits in the observation room, reaching to turn the probe in a circle, three hundred and sixty degrees, swinging momentarily past the ground they've gained. If she does it too often, the team back in BC will notice and call to check in—or, more specifically, to chastise her for slowing progress. If done only rarely, however, a paused and circling probe won't signal a significant loss in time. The movement will go unnoticed.

It's during one of these rare circlings that she sees it, retreating from the light, shrinking away like lightning running backward, its body white and oddly shaped, bumpy, swollen with growths.

* * * *

SHE'S DREAMING, but she doesn't know it yet.

In her dream, she feels the hurrying expansion of *already*, like something invisible rushing fast at her from the future. Already she can feel her daughter's hair falling from her head. She has the thought again (when has she had it before?) that her daughter is growing backward. Her daughter is sitting on a stool on the back porch, and she is brushing her hair. They are both looking out at the yard. Her daughter's loose hair is so blond that it looks silvery in her hands, tangling with her fingers as she pulls them away. Already she can see patches of skin appearing like shadows on her daughter's scalp.

In the back of the yard there is sunshine, and the raspberry bushes are swaying.

She wakes in a thunder to her bed in the middle of the night, her mind shouldering into consciousness with an ache that she doesn't at first recognize as grief swelling in her chest.

Already—in her dream she had been thrown back into the *already*.

* * * *

IT ISN'T difficult to locate the fish once they know that it exists. They occasionally turn the cameras around, according to her suggestion, and find the fish is following them, weaving at a distance behind in the water. They take photographs, zoom in, and study its enlarged face. They decide this will be the zenith of their careers, the discovery that will place their names in textbooks after they're dead. She's tired from sitting in the observation room and isn't sure she cares about peaks anymore—about estimating or reaching potentials. But she looks at the photographs and realizes before the rest of them what the growths covering the fish's body are.

They're eyes, she says, squinting down at the tablet in her hand.

What? says Anthony. He slides his wheeled chair over from across the room.

It doesn't have any scales, she says. No fins. I can't even see gills. It's covered in eyes.

She traces a white bulge on the screen with her fingertip.

Let me see, he says, holding out his hand. They can't be eyes. They just *look* like eyes.

She hands him the tablet. Compare the photographs, she says. The pupils change direction.

He stares down at the pictures. It would be unprecedented, he says. It would be impossible.

Their zenith soars higher above them. In a week, they catch the fish.

* * * *

WAIT, she says. The word crackles in her throat, caught on a bubble of phlegm. She hiccups through her breathlessness. Wait.

They don't wait. The trap snaps down around the fish, the thin wire edges—she sees them through the cameras—closing on its gliding body. The head has been caught, sure enough, the eyeballs careening in their numerous sockets, but the latter half of the fish, its long, eel-like tail, has been cut, deeply. It twists as if electrocuted, thrashing and pulling against the cage.

It opens its mouth. She wonders, not for the first time, if fish can scream—if they feel a desire to scream. The fish's mouth is long and oval at the front of its face, and inside, deep inside the dark pocket of mouth that stretches down to its throat, she thinks but isn't sure she sees the swell of white growths shining in the camera lights.

More eyes, and on the inside of its mouth? What's the use in that? What evolutionary process, hard-edged and traceable as a mathematical equation, led to this fish growing eyes on the inside of its mouth?

The fleshy gums of the fish's lips, red like the undersides of large eyelids, angle toward the camera. It's not screaming, she thinks. It's looking.

Then the cage snaps upward, the fish's mouth snaps shut, and the camera remains recording empty sand and rock and shadow.

Wait, she says again, this time under her breath. They're up on deck, on the top of the water, and overboard in the deep she can see the ropes straining, retracting upward to pull the cage into view. The metal wiring emerges from the water. The fish is writhing inside of it. Its tail, black with blood and slippery, hangs half-detached and motionless outside the cage. A single, pale eyeball at the end of its tail is limp and dead, white and quickly drying out in the open air.

She stares for a moment at this eyeball, its black pupil blank and turning milky with blindness. The head of the fish, blistered with eyeballs of all sizes, thumps against the metal cage.

The others don't have time to react. They're preparing

for extraction, donning rubber gloves and wheeling over the aquarium, writing numbers in the charts of their clipboards. She steps forward as the cage reaches eye level, snaps open the locks, and reaches for the fish with her bare hands. Her fingers close around the eyeballs. They're smooth and firm like hard-boiled eggs on her skin.

The others lurch toward her. There's blood, sticky and wet, between her fingers. She hears the rattle of supplies hitting the deck and the splash of the fish as it hits the water and disappears.

Anthony shakes her brutally until she thinks her neck will snap.

2

In her dreams, in her memories, which are the same now, more or less the same, she's standing on the back porch looking into the house. It's dark inside the house—she can barely see the outline of the kitchen counter and the refrigerator and the chairs. The outlines of furniture are dim, blurring into shadow, shapes emerging momentarily from the darkness like fish underwater. She finds herself straining to see if there are little blue polka-dotted boots by the back door. This is a staple of time, a stamp, a certification. If the blue polka-dotted boots are by the back door, then there must be feet to put into them. There must be a little body somewhere very close, surely within sight, or just out of sight, at the corner of her eye. Her vision smudges with darkness, a smear of ashen charcoal behind her eyelids. She is dreaming, after all.

She strains to see, but even in her straining she knows that she's wasting her time looking for these polka-dotted boots. Behind her, if she could just turn around, her daughter crouches at the back of the yard, way back through the grass and between the flowers bobbing their heads in the breeze. She's crouching in the grass, barefoot, reaching into a tangle of thorny bush, plucking raspberries that lean in through the fence from the neighboring yard. She knows that if she could turn around she would see her daughter scooping the front of her dress into a bowl to carry the raspberries, her lips and chin and fingertips stained dark red, as if bruised, her hair soft and falling around her face (not falling out, not yet, not *already*), blades of grass coming up between her toes, dirt on her kneecaps from where they pressed into the earth.

Stubbornly she stares into the dark interior of the kitchen, watching for the revelation of household objects, the shape of the wall, the spiraling metal rings of the stove.

* * * *

SIX DAYS after she loses her job and goes back to her house that she never sold but always meant to, she finds a bulge on the back of her neck, in the crook between the base of her skull and the top of her spinal column. It's painful, sore like a raised zit, and she pokes it experimentally throughout the day. By evening, it's the size of a small egg, firm like stiff jelly beneath the skin.

She calls her mother, whom she realizes mid-ring she hasn't told about losing her job.

About time! says her mother. You know it's been ages, don't you? Your father and I started watching the news for a story about a flooded submarine. I told him the other day, I said, I don't know how she can stand that job, way down at the bottom of the ocean. It's about time she called us, and it's about time she came back up to the world of the living for good.

She listens for a moment to the static hum of her cell phone. It's quiet down there, she says. Mostly. She thinks of Anthony.

Well, says her mother, this is another one of your breaks, I guess? Have they put you up in a hotel like usual? It's awful living in hotels part-time and on a boat the rest. It can't be healthy. You always have a home with us, you know. You should come up for dinner tomorrow night, if you're near enough. Your father bought some steaks, and I'm making asparagus. It won't be an inconvenience to have you. It's always good to have you.

I'm far away, she says. She stammers, We—we've landed far up the coast.

Shame, says her mother. She pauses, deliberating. That's not a life, you know. That's no kind of life.

Is Dad there? she asks. I could talk to Dad, if he's around.

He's in bed, her mother says.

Oh. She thinks about hanging up the phone.

Her mother breathes. I know I've said it before, and I'll say it again. It's not healthy. It's not any kind of life. It's time you came back up and started living. It's been five years since the funeral and that's long enough for anyone. I know this job felt right at the time, but five years is plenty enough time to get your head the right way on your shoulders again. We miss her too, you know. You're not the only one out there in the world who's ever lost a child. I said to your father the other day, I said, time doesn't turn around for anyone, and if she thinks—

She hangs up the phone and places it on the kitchen counter, staring at her dark reflection in its rectangular face. In the silence, her fingers move involuntarily up to the lump—which feels larger now—on the back of her head.

* * * *

WHEN SHE balances the smaller mirror from her bedroom on top of the back of the toilet, positioned so that, when she looks in the bathroom mirror, she can see the back of her head—when she ties up her hair and looks in the bathroom mirror and pushes the knife into the skin at the base of her skull—she expects fluid and pus but gets neither. Instead, she slices, pulls the skin, and sees a pupil in the center of a white eyeball on the back of her head.

She is looking into both mirrors now, from the front and the back, a kaleidoscope of reflections colliding. She vomits into the sink, tries to blink, and feels the skin on the back of her neck pulling together like a clenched fist.

Vertigo rocks through her as she moves out of the bathroom and into the kitchen, walking simultaneously forward and backward, watching the hallway slide under her as in the same moment it slides away.

* * * *

THE NEXT lump appears behind her left ear, and the next just above her forehead, in her hairline. She cuts each open with meticulous precision. She learns to balance—she can move around the house without issue—and she wonders now how she ever moved before, her head thumping with the revelation not only of all that she can see but also of all that she can possibly not see—all the absences of points of view that she didn't feel until these additional ones arose.

With each new eye, more hair falls from her head. She shaves off all that's left over, as if in invitation.

* * * *

SHE DREAMS that looking from behind herself she can see her daughter sitting on a stool on the porch having her hair brushed by a woman who is looking away toward the back of the yard. Her daughter's hair is falling out as the woman brushes, already silvery in the woman's hands. And beneath the hair, where the pale shadows form already, are eyeballs breaking out against the skin. As the eyelids, which are also the skin of her daughter's scalp, clench shut, they squeeze the hair from their pores, and it tangles in silvery strands between the woman's fingers as she draws her hands away.

In the dream, the woman turns and looks at her where she stands looking from behind herself, looking from inside the back of her neck. They look at each other.

The woman opens her mouth, an oval wideness in her face. In the dark cavity of her scream there are white lumps swiveling on her tongue.

* * * *

WHEN ANTHONY CALLS, she's in the kitchen looking into the fridge and in the same moment looking at the ceiling where a crack forms a spiderweb constellation in the plaster and in the same moment looking out the glass back door to the porch and the yard and the sun scooping down through the sky.

She's gentle when she places the phone to her ear.

It's Anthony, says Anthony.

Hello, she says.

How've you been?

The phone hums for a moment into her head. Why're you calling? she asks.

We found it again.

She can hear it now—there's an edge to his voice. He's breathing sharply, as if he's just run up a flight of stairs.

Did you catch it? she asks. Her tongue feels numb in her mouth.

Of course, he says, but it's not the same one. At least, we don't think it's the same one. We're fairly sure it's not the same one.

What do you mean?

Well, there's a scar.

A scar?

On its tail. The eyeballs are damaged in a full circumference around its tail exactly where—

Ah, she says, pulling the details together in her mind. And no one believes you. That's why you've called?

Well, do you think it's possible?

That it healed itself? She reaches her hands up to her head, touching the folds of skin pinching around her eyes. She closes them all at once. In darkness, she can think.

And she thinks that there's an edge to his voice. He's breathing sharply, as if he's just run up a flight of stairs. They don't believe him. What experiment will they require as proof?

No, she says. It's not possible. It's not possible even in reptiles, you know that. The tail was dead. We all saw it. I had the—the—she stammers, losing some of her composure—the blood on my hands to prove it.

But what if this is different? he asks. What if we should be thinking about this differently?

You'll lose your job, she says, if you kill it. If you're wrong, you'll lose your job.

This is enough for him to consent. She hears the breath piling out of his lungs.

He pauses, unsure of how to say he doesn't need her anymore. How've you been? he asks again.

Her hands move up to her head.

* * * *

SHE'S BEEN WELL, she's been nothing, she's been well.

She's well, she's nothing, nothing matters about well in the nothing that inhabits her brain. She's now, in the space between not yet and *already* and since. In the space between the not yet here and the already happening and the since then, the afterward, what she used to call now. Now the now sees forward and backward. Her head is hairless and bumpy with eyeballs. She sits on the back porch, looking out into the yard, and behind her in the dark interior of the kitchen the shapes of furniture loom and surface like the shapes of fish underwater. Now the now sees forward and backward. She sees her daughter in the bed of the hospital and hairless, she sees her daughter in the bed of the coffin. She sees the fish slipping backward like lightning retracting. And the blood of the fish in between her fingers, slipping in between the in-between of *already*. She sees her daughter tiny on her chest in the hospital, finding her breast with her mouth and then sleeping, her fingers sticky with blood. She sees her daughter eating Cheerios. She sees her daughter standing on the piano in the living room humming "Angel of Music" from *The Phantom of the Opera* as she chimes notes with her toes and tries to climb inside. She sees her red face facedown in the carpet, mad that it's school time—she slept in too long—and her eyes still hold the puff beneath them from her dreams. She wonders what she was dreaming. Was she dreaming of going back to sleep? Now the now sees forward and backward. She sees her daughter in the bed of the coffin. She sees her daughter trying to walk down the stairs and holding the banister. She sees her toes in the bathtub wrinkled, emerging from the water like pruned eyeballs at the ends of her feet. Now in the now the fish is swimming backward. She turns the camera backward and sees the fish opening its mouth. She sees the pouch of dreaming beneath her daughter's eyes. Her daughter is hairless and dreaming in the hospital bed—she's a baby, it's the first, she's grown—she kisses her. The beginning and end fold together like dough, pouched dough like skin pouched together under the eyes.

She sees her daughter coming up from the back of the yard.

Mama, look, the little girl says, holding out her hand. It's an offering, an invitation. Her fingers are dark red, as if bruised. On her palm is a raspberry, plump, pulled from the bush at the back of the yard. On her palm is her mother's head, hairless and bumpy with eyeballs, tiny, small enough to sit in her palm—a sphere of thick lumps. She brings it to her mouth and whispers in its ear.

Mama, look.

WHEN NELLIE LOOKS UP from the words she has been reading in Husha's mother's book, she sees that Husha is crying and can't breathe.

Homogeneous Nothing

THE HOLE ARRIVED WITH THE HEAT, but no one suspected the connection except Tillie, who threw her hand over her nose and said, The hole is breathing. I can taste its breath.

If the hole really were breathing, if *breathing* was the word to best describe the slow, consistent leak of air from its deep belly, then its breath was hot. It had been a warm summer already, the end of June leaning back into its beginning, opening its arms into the final days of May, and now the heat—mid-July—was nearly impenetrable, hanging like an invisible wall outside every closed and air-conditioned front door. The heat at the cottage was better, but it was still bad. From the sunbaked driveway, between the pine trees and carefully sectioned-off underbrush, to the edge of the windless lake where the dock and the boats bobbed disconsolately with their reflections, the heat wedged itself, thick, wet, and pressing, into the air.

The heat was almost enough to distract from the hole, which arrived, as Tillie noticed, on the same day.

The hole was in the driveway, so it was hard to ignore. The hole was in the driveway, so it swallowed the car first. Peter was the first to find the car missing when he went outside to drive to the marina and pick up his morning newspaper, an anachronism he still entertained while on holiday at the cottage. It was a whimsical act, this buying and reading of the newspaper, an act that made him feel nostalgic for his boyhood and lazy Sunday mornings spent in the kitchen with his mother. Besides, he reasoned (he reasoned with the rational part of his brain), the local

Erica McKeen

economy deserved his business, and there was something that struck him as pleasing, something quaint and almost laughable, in the way the owners of the marina—a husband and wife widely set, with dark eyebrows angling down toward the bridges of their noses as if they were siblings—sniffed at him when they thought he wasn't looking, passing a word between them as if they knew something he had as yet failed to recognize.

He always paid for the paper by credit card. He liked the feeling of plastic sliding against leather when he pulled the card from his wallet. He liked the look of the generous tip he added to his total on the machine.

But this morning, when he went out the back door of the cottage, pulling his keys prematurely from his pocket, Peter found the car missing and a hole there instead. The hole was roughly circular and reached either side of the driveway. It was deep, impossibly deep—Peter couldn't lean far enough over to see the bottom.

Peter's daughter, Tillie, threw her hand over her nose. She was standing in the open bathroom window, her dress hiked up over her knees, almost to her hips, because she had just been preparing to pee when she saw her dad outside staring into the hole.

It stinks, she said, her voice strangled through her fingers. Peter didn't hear her. He didn't smell anything, either, despite his head hanging over the mouth of the hole. All he felt, throughout his entire body, was the heat.

Like mud, Tillie said. Like rotten mud.

Later she would change her description, when they all stood around the edge of the hole, staring into its center, not venturing too close for fear of erosion. Peter, Martha (Peter's wife, wringing her wrists with her hands), Old Peter (Peter's father, rub-

82

bery jowls hanging, in transition to a nursing home, this time at the cottage existing as a temporary arrangement because Peter hadn't found an appropriate placement for him yet, everything too ill-kept or unorganized, every home, even the expensive ones, too imprecise), Little Peter (Peter's son, already collecting stones and pinecones to throw into the hole, already eyeing his sister's hair to pull), Tillie (hair in curls, a tempting poof around her head, and yellow dress jam-stained—Martha examining it between glances at the hole, exasperated, counting the laundry loads), and Toad (their French bulldog, saggy-lipped, with brindle fur and a limp, one slouching red eye; only Tillie called her Toad, this is what she had named her from the beginning, but everyone else knew her as Joanne).

Peter, Martha, Old Peter, Little Peter, Tillie, and Toad/Joanne.

Together, they looked into the hole. Tillie was the first to speak. It was a reverent moment, this collective looking, and she knew that, she could feel it—something prehistoric and colossal in the way the earth fell off into darkness in front of them. The others in the family felt a wordlessness curling like smoke in their heads, but Tillie couldn't help herself. She had a problem with holding her tongue.

It stinks, she said.

Little Peter's neck snapped around in reflex. *You* stink, he retorted, scrunching up his nose.

Quiet! hissed Martha. She was a practiced yoga instructor and, as a result, had a special relationship with reverence, didn't like to interrupt it.

Toad/Joanne grunted and sighed, sat back in the dirt with her hind legs sticking out straight in front of her.

Some kind of earthquake, mumbled Peter.

Mm hm, said Old Peter, nodding sedately, only having half-heard what his son had said.

Separately, too, they looked into the hole.

To Peter, the hole looked like an obstacle, something that, in his boyhood, he might have liked to jump across. Or climb into. Its openness was like an invitation, a space for him to fill.

To Martha, the hole looked like the dark scoop at the bottom of anxiety.

Old Peter could hardly see the hole, although he looked in the same direction that the others looked. He hadn't told anyone yet, but he had begun to go blind.

To Little Peter, the hole looked like something he wanted to hurt. It had frustratingly swallowed everyone's attention. He had already thrown one stone into it—the sharpest he could find—and, even more alarmingly, absolutely nothing had happened. The stone disappeared, the hole didn't flinch, and his family kept staring.

To Tillie, in her bare feet and big eyes, the hole looked open

like a wide-open mouth
between words that
against. It hol-
in her head the
does, sluggish
like the slack
couldn't quite
her head commanded.

hollowed out like a gap
the brain splinters
lowed out a space
same way heat
and immobilizing,
bones in her limbs
catch hold of what
The hole was heat in the

way it stunted thought and motion. It was epistemological nothing, the separation between Tillie and *Tillie*, herself and *herself*, Tillie and the outside that was not Tillie, aching her with hurt like the sloughing pain in a separated shoulder.

Hand still over her nose, Tillie changed her description. Out of respect, she changed her description. Not *it stinks*. Not *like rotten mud*. But instead, *The hole is breathing. I can taste its breath.*

To Toad/Joanne, the hole looked like anything else. She licked her lips in the sauna heat of its exhalation.

* * * *

BY LUNCHTIME, three trees had sagged as if in exhaustion and collapsed into the hole. The hole had undoubtedly widened. Its circumference crumbled toward the bottom porch step.

And the heat had undoubtedly thickened. It had undoubtedly deepened. Cellphone service at the cottage was always sporadic, but now it had completely disappeared (into the hole—the heat?), and Peter declared he would walk to the marina to contact the authorities if service didn't return in an hour.

An hour? said Martha. They were standing in the living room by the large bay windows that looked out toward the lake. From the corner of her eye, Martha could see Little Peter teetering around the kitchen with a damp washcloth balanced on his forehead. Old Peter sat in a chair by the front door with his head hanging down between his shoulders. Tillie and Toad/Joanne were nowhere to be seen.

An hour? she repeated. Shouldn't we—

Shouldn't *we*? Peter cut in. (Martha wrung her hands.) Will *we* be walking to the marina, or will *I* be walking to the marina?

The trees swayed mutely on the other side of the window glass.

And if *I* am walking to the marina, he continued unheeded,

ignoring the fact that Martha would not look at him, I'm sure that *I* can make the decision about when is best to go.

He paced around the room twice in long, purposeful strides, his arms crossed over his chest, circling the carved, artisanal stump that served as their coffee table. Finally he looked up and saw Martha's expression, the deep wrinkle between her eyebrows, and softened, as he always—inevitably, eventually—did. He assured her that an hour was the longest he would wait. An hour was all he needed in order to rest, because the heat had made him drowsy, the heat had made his thoughts slow and uncertain. He would just close his eyes for a moment, only for a moment lie on the couch and watch Martha huff and sigh and leave the room, close his eyes against the heat—and three hours later he woke to Little Peter poking him in the face where he lay with his head pinned between the cushions and his shirt soaked through with sweat.

In the meantime, the hole had swallowed the shed that stood beside the cottage, the shed that held the water skis and wakeboard and life jackets and canoe oars. The hole had pulled off the porch steps.

Dad, said Little Peter. Dad, Dad, Dad, Dad, Dad.

Tillie was in the garden with Toad/Joanne, digging smaller holes no more than ten feet away from the big one, pushing her fingers into the earth. Martha saw her from the sunroom at the side of the cottage, where she was reclining in sweat in a rocking chair. Without lifting an eyebrow, she said, Tillie, can you hear me? Get inside right now. I told you not to play so close to that hole. Tillie? Tillie, now, you listen to me.

Tillie didn't react to her mother's whisper falling through the screen window. Both she and Toad/Joanne were more accustomed, and therefore more responsive, to Martha's yell.

But God it was *hot*, and Martha had no energy to yell. She had no energy even to move. It was *hot* and the lake water did nothing to help. It had begun to bake and had begun to smell, too, like a bucket of urine. The fans set up around the cottage did nothing. They provided no more than a warm beating of breath on Martha's skin. The open windows did nothing. They made it worse. The air was stagnant, moldering (it was palpable to the point that it could complete the process of moldering). And there was no air conditioning. This was something Martha had decided when they built the cottage (or, rather, when they paid someone to build the cottage for them), that they would have no air conditioning. It's sometimes nice, she had reasoned (she reasoned with the rational part of her brain)—and in a rare moment of harmony Peter had agreed—sometimes nice to have less in order to experience more, to do without some common conveniences and feel the reality of, for example, the outside air filtering into your home. They left the city to escape schedules, to escape obligations and regulations, and a regulated air temperature seemed too indicative of this lifestyle, the numbers on the thermostat too exact and unyielding. There was something liberating in letting the world for once take care of itself. This was the same ideology that made her fight off the installation of the internet for so long. Less convenience denoted a more natural and therefore more appealing state of living—it meant quiet, it meant fresh air and time spent out of doors. It was a battle Martha constantly and diligently undertook, the good fight, the wholesome struggle for less.

So the air in the cottage began to regurgitate itself, moving in humid slurps in and out of the family's lungs.

* * * *

DAD, said Little Peter, poking his father in his flabby cheek. Dad, Dad, Dad, Dad, Dad.

* * * *

TILLIE WAS in the garden. Tillie was in the tall grass by the swampy side pocket of the lake. Tillie was beneath the basement stairs, rummaging for paint so she could color the canoe. Tillie was in the crook of a tree, her dress pulled up around her waist, letting the heat slide by her legs.

Tillie was standing beside the rocking chair in the sunroom. Mom, she said. Martha woke wondering where the light had gone. It was the middle of the night.

Mom, said Tillie. Where's Grandpa?

Martha felt sludge in her head that she was sure would slide out her ears when she stood up. She moved Tillie aside with one arm and went to the living room, glancing at the empty chair by the front door. She woke Little Peter and Peter, who had fallen asleep together on the couch, Little Peter's face pasted and drooling onto his father's wet shirt.

Martha shook Peter by his shoulder harder than she consciously intended.

Where's Grandpa? Where's your father?

Peter sat up, swiveling his head around on top of his neck. The cottage was dark. Old Peter was nowhere. His shoes were gone too.

I'm going to the marina, said Peter.

Martha said, It's the middle of the night.

I have my wallet, said Peter, and my cellphone. He held them up like weapons. He pulled on his sandals and opened the back door to find the hole waiting for his first step. It had swallowed the porch leading down to the driveway, all of it. Peter went out the front instead, toward the lake, and circled around to the forest. And was gone.

Martha was standing at the open back door, wringing her hands and staring down into the hole. We should go find some flashlights, she said to no one in particular. In case the power goes out.

She went down to the basement and sat in the corner of the room.

Upstairs, Toad/Joanne reclined on the carpet, sloppily licking her paws. Tillie had turned on a lamp and found a book to read off the bookshelf. The heat had wrinkled the pages, and she tried to smooth them with her fingertips. Little Peter, looking sour and tired, yanked the utensil drawer out from under the counter in the kitchen and stood by the open back door, chucking spoons into the black and vacuous hole. The humidity had struck him like a hammer striking bone, and each throw swung his exhausted body dangerously over the edge.

Little son-of-a—he muttered, hurling a butter knife. He tossed tablespoons and steak knives and tiny silver forks meant to spear small pickles and portions of smoked meat. Stupid little no-good-piece-of—

In her book, the pages of which were smattered with lamplight, illustrated with birds in flight, Tillie had discovered a chapter explaining the bone density of loons.

We could camp out by the lake, she said, flipping a page.

But nobody—no nothing—was listening.

It would be good to get some rest, she said. The heat won't let us rest.   But nobody was listening.

Her eyelids began to fold like curtains over her face. We could leave on the boat, she said. Get as far away as possible. But nobody—no nothing, no nothing—was listening. The cottage was quiet, and Little Peter had disappeared from the doorstep.

* * * *

IN THE MORNING, when dim, gray light had begun to push up at the edges of the sky, Toad/Joanne and Tillie went down to the water. It was the only place Tillie thought they might be safe, because the water belonged to nobody. Even Peter had admitted once, while driving his family around the lake in dizzying spirals in the speedboat, that the water belonged to nobody. You can buy all the land around it, he said, and still someone can drop down from the sky and into the lake and be perfectly within their rights. It was a riddle he couldn't decipher, a puzzle he couldn't put together. He knew, at least, that it had something to do with movement, that the movement of the water was unmanageable—that there was something enigmatic in its simplicity, its liquid homogeneity, that would always resist possession. There was something as elusive as emptiness, something as slippery as heat, in its sustained, unvarying fluidity.

Tillie went to the water and waded in up to her knees. Her yellow dress bloomed around her, wet, like a sunspot in the dark morning.

Toad/Joanne whimpered.

Tillie waited.

Martha, in the basement, deep now in the basement of herself, found that she couldn't feel the sweat on her forehead anymore. Her hands were numb. She experienced a moment of relief, of bliss and coolness, like an icy wind against her skin, and she wondered if this was what her meditation books were trying to teach her. Breathe in, breathe out. Picture a sunny beach with light coming through the trees and waves lapping. Even if you're already on a sunny beach with light coming through the trees, picture it. Martha exhaled. A sudden stillness, a total freezing nothingness snaked up through the bones in her toes. Lessness, openness, emptiness.

She opened her eyes and saw that the floor was gone in front of her.

* * * *

As the sun rose higher, a breeze started up from across the lake and pulled through the heat like fingers pulling through hair. Goose bumps stuck up on Tillie's forearms as she walked through the bushes. She felt the insistent tug of twigs on the fabric of her dress. The cottage was gone. It was as if it had never been. Tillie could see all the way back to the start of the forest.

She and Toad (no longer Joanne) sat on the edge of the hole. Toad sniffed the air and smiled and Tillie swung her legs and swung her legs and swung her legs and swung her legs and swung

It's their second night of reading, and Husha has recovered the ability to speak. The living room is dark: there is a light on in the hallway, back behind the kitchen, emanating a soft orange hue, and a tea-light candle burns low on the coffee table, its flame blushing purple against the grainy dregs of two glasses of red wine. Arthur has propped his feet up beside the glasses, and Nellie lies horizontal on the couch.

I had a dream, says Husha from where she sits on the carpet, leaning against Arthur's chair, that I was—

She sees Nellie's expression, her head turned sideways against the couch cushion, and pauses.

What? asks Husha.

What? says Nellie. Nothing!

What's that face for, that look?

What look?

Well, it's gone now.

Just continue with your story.

Is the dream thing too worn out? Too cliché? I've just been having a lot of them lately. She leans forward against the coffee table and drops her chin into her hand.

If you keep having them, says Nellie, I guess they can't be worn out.

Arthur interjects: Like I've told you before, I think they're stuck in the walls.

Nellie angles her head to look up at him. She rolls to her side, the shadow of a smile dimpling her cheeks as she reaches over to pat his hand, settled delicately on the armrest of his chair.

It's an interesting idea, she says.

Oh! Arthur scowls. Don't patronize me. He fidgets, trying to readjust his legs. I'm not one to believe in the supernatural. It's speculation at most. It's the idea that a certain energy in a space can—influence—a sensitive person's subconscious.

Sounds more supernatural than speculative to me, says Nellie, but she laughs kindly as she speaks. Didn't you work as a scientist? she asks. Wasn't your entire job based in empiricism?

Arthur shrugs. I was a professor of plant pathology. And if I learned anything from plants, it's that invisible forces— sunlight, wind pressure, some minute ingredient in the soil— can vastly alter development.

So you're saying there's something in the soil? asks Husha, thinking again of the cicadas digging themselves out of the ground.

The soil, says Arthur. The walls. The air. Haven't either of you had strange dreams since you came here?

The three sit in silence for a moment, each reflecting on his or her nighttime visions. Husha is what one might call a frequent dreamer, a restless sleeper. It isn't unusual for her, regardless of her surroundings, to dream four or five times a week, but she has to admit that her dreams since arriving at the house have been particularly vivid. Opaque. Solid like recent memory. She doesn't attribute it to the architectural structure of the house—something lodged in the wood of the walls, for example, or buried under the floorboards—but rather to the psychological situation of being in the house, that the house is a place she spent time in as a child with her mother and grandparents, a core family locale. Now her mother has died and here Husha is, inhabiting this same space of summer escape under entirely different circumstances. The mental discordance between peaceful memory and present-day discomfort must be the root of her hallucinations (because the dreams do feel almost like hallucinations) instead of some transparent substance in the walls.

It's not proof of anything, though, is it? says Nellie, who has personally never had so many dreams in her life as she does regularly now, each night.

Not proof, no, says Arthur. But I think it's worth our consideration.

It was clearly something your mother considered, says Nellie, addressing Husha. She bumps the book with her elbow, which lies flat between them on the coffee table. Have you looked at "Anne, Cassandra, and the Sleep House"?

You've read ahead? asks Husha. She looks at Nellie, her ludicrous half-smile fading against the couch cushion. Nellie's hands rise up sideways in defense, or perhaps protection. Husha feels stung, the inside of her throat growing furry with frustration as she tries to speak.

Not read ahead, not really, says Nellie quickly. Just glanced.

Glanced, repeats Husha.

I didn't know the rules! Nellie sounds exasperated. I was perusing.

Perusing.

Okay, says Arthur softly. He has pulled his feet off the coffee table.

Husha closes her eyes. She puts her hands over her face, listening to the leather crinkle of the couch as Nellie changes position, to the sound of Arthur's loose, tumbling breaths. She feels simultaneously numb with rage and childish for becoming so angry so rapidly, so unaccountably.

Okay, says her grandfather again. Listen. Didn't we agree the book was for everyone? And I doubt Nellie—he glances at her—will do it again. Can we assume there was no mal intent?

In fact, there might have been good intent, Nellie cuts in. I was trying to ensure—

She looks up at the ceiling, searching for the right phrase.

Ensure what? Husha asks, releasing the words on an exhalation, exhausted.

Ensure there was nothing horrific ahead. Considering your mother's potential state of mind while writing.

Husha spreads her fingers across her cheekbones, and then smooths them down to her neck. She holds the base of her shoulders, blowing out her lips in a long sigh.

Should we read some more? she asks.

You still haven't told us about your dream, Nellie points out.

Right, says Husha. You really want to hear it?

Her grandfather settles back in his chair. Nellie, sitting up now on the couch, folds her hands expectantly in her lap, like an eager kid in a classroom. Husha laughs.

Okay, she begins. You'll have to tell me what to make of it.

* * * *

IN HER dream she's sitting in her grandfather's chair. The living room is dark, lights out, the fireplace dull ash. There's a shape on the couch across from her, but she can't tell if it's a person or a clump of blankets. She senses that it's very late, the middle of the night. She hears a sound coming from the other side of the room, from the back door, a sound like a stick hitting glass. *The trees are bending down and trying to get my attention*, she thinks.

In her dream she gets up from the chair and walks across the room to the back door. Her legs have trouble moving, as if they've been sewn together at the thighs, so it takes her a while, her footsteps fumbling, to reach the door and the sound of continual tapping, tapping, tapping. When she opens the door she discovers that it's night but she can see everything. The colors have flipped, reversed, like a camera shooting in negative. The trees and ground are white and the sky is black.

In her dream a giant cicada stands upright on the back step. It's as tall as a human and wide, almost filling her field of vision. She stares at its hard, black belly, metallic sockets shining where the legs protrude. The legs wave softly as if in a slow wind. She stares at its stiff, tucked glass wings.

In her dream a sound like screeching tires fills the air. She can feel her ears bleeding. Something is wrong with the cicada's head. It takes her a moment to register the error. In her dream at the top of the cicada's body is her grandfather's face, flush with the insect's shoulders, gazing placidly upward at the black sky, like a mask plastered, lifeless and unconcerned.

Mouth

Hands [1]

are in her lap as she settles herself on the edge of the bed. Her finger pads hold the same whorls from when she was younger. In the stairwell there is a photograph of herself at fifteen. It wasn't unusual at that time to die of certain fevers and strains of pneumonia, certain bacterial infections, and in the picture she had been dying. Her brother took it—obtrusively. She vaguely remembers that in the blur of her illness came a flash and her brother scurrying away, and her mother flying after him, and in recovery she requested the photo and kept it, and kept the sketches he had made of her too.

Hands [2]

She used both [2] hands to frame the photograph and hang it on the wall in the stairwell, so each night before going to bed she would see it.

Hands [3]

Her daughter, Colleen, didn't like the photograph, and on her way up to bed she would rush with both her [2] hands covering her eyes. When she reached the top she would go to her mother and pull her [1] large hand onto her skin, pressing it like a warm washcloth, [3] hands in layers swallowing her face.

Face [1]

Facing her mother, who sits on the edge of the bed and faces away from her, looking toward the open doorway and the stairwell beyond, Colleen unties the laces of one thick black shoe. Although she unties the laces expertly, pulling the shoe from the sock and the rubber skin of her mother's blocklike foot, she's thinking of other things—of her husband at home and the children's shoes she will tie in the morning, discarding this one last duty of the day already into her memory, this final and repetitive act of putting her mother to bed, looking onward to the next serviceable motion of these her [2] hands, the many accommodating expressions she will plant upon her face.

Looking away from her, holding her face in profile, her mother is in the middle of telling her a story.

Little toy cars, she says, on the top of the step, lined up like they were in a traffic jam.

Little toy cars? asks Colleen. You know how this makes you sound.

Of course I know how it makes me sound. I can hear myself, can't I? But that's what happened, that's what I saw: little toy cars, on the top of the step, lined up like they were in a traffic jam. All different colors, but instead of wheels they had feet.

God, Mom!

All in a row, all different colors.

This is the kind of stuff that would make a normal daughter put you away in a nursing home, you know. You're just lucky— —that I raised you myself and taught you better than that?

Face [1—mouth (1)]

No, what I was going to say was that you're just lucky I don't have the money to put you away anywhere fancy. I couldn't in good conscience put you away anywhere less than fancy because I'm sure—I'm *sure*—you would drive whatever roommate they cramped you in with to her semi-premature death.

What—because of my talking?

I would call it more your *mouth*.

Ha! You don't know how good you have it. All of this—she gestures to the dim bedroom, the clutter in the corners, the smell of something between disinfectant and decay, the bed on which she perches, Colleen crouched before her, untying her shoes—would be much less exciting without *my mouth* for entertainment.

Well, close your mouth for one minute, would you? Hold still.

Colleen leans her shoulder against the side of the bed, pulling off the second shoe with the care necessary to not stretch the flesh on the swollen slope around the Achilles' tendon. Her mother sighs and flexes her toes.

Body [1]

Looking at the photo her brother had taken of her while she was dying, and all of the sketches based off the photograph, she

99

grew alarmed at the precise delineation of her face. The single pencil marking that shaped the length of her nose was sharp and exact. The sockets of her eyes were shaded into tenebrous realism, and her chin seemed to struggle against the confines of the paper, seemed to push, bony, off the page. Her cheekbones were angular with emaciation. Her body, in contrast, was consistently vague, her limbs swathed in blankets, formless, like the mucus inside a cocoon. This vagueness soothed her; it felt suitable, accurate in its uncertainty. The presumption behind the repetitive, precise faces seemed to be that death could be captured and categorized—that it could be segmented, pulled apart. She knew this was the wrong approach to take, but maybe the only possible one, for representation's sake.

From her near death she learned that dying is messy and sloppy, as uncoordinated as a baby deer.

Body [2]

Colleen was ashamed at first to help her mother undress. But the nobility of her mother's posture as she pulled off her shirt and unclipped her bra, even with her bent back, turned something over in Colleen, like turning over a stone and discovering a brightly speckled salamander instead of earthworms, like hauling a weight off a pocket of cool air and allowing it, like breath, to escape. It was important to witness her mother in nudity. She realized after seeing the length of her mother's wrinkled breasts that she had been less ashamed than afraid: afraid of solidifying within her mind the form that her own body would one day inhabit. It was the fear of her middle-aged body [1] overlapping and coinciding with that of her elderly mother's [2], creating a sort of slipstream in which she became not herself.

Body [3]

In her memories later, in her dreams that are also memories, Colleen will find herself stumbling through sheets of flesh strung up like laundry on a line. Behind these sheets she will see the shadow of the third body, the complete and separate body [3] made from the amalgamation of her own and her mother's.

She will stumble through the sheets, groping after this shadow.

Face [1—mouth (2)]

Colleen is laughing.

Some of the toenails on the little feet were painted, says her mother.

Some of them had little designs—pedicures.

The laughter falls like small pieces of voice out of Colleen's mouth:

ha

 ha

  ha

 ha

ha

ha

ha

ha

ha

ha

ha

ha

ha

and the only reason she doesn't keep laughing across the room and back again, her voice marching along the walls, is because her mother begins to slip ever steadily off the side of the bed (there is no muscle, no fat left at the top of her thighs to secure her tailbone on the blanket). Colleen stands up, one smooth, serious movement, like an ax swinging to its mark, hooks her mother under the armpits, and heaves her, squatting like a weightlifter, back onto the bed.

It's a wonder you haven't broken a hip, says Colleen.

I'm tired, says her mother. You're the one taking so long to get me out of these clothes.

Face [1—mouth (3)]

Finish that story you were telling me.

I thought you didn't like it.

I thought it was ridiculous. I never said I didn't like it.

Sure, okay, but no more interruptions.

. . .

What's that for?

What?

That face.

What face? This is me not interrupting you.

You've never made things easy, have you?

Come *on*, Mom.

Do you want me to tell the story or not?

What do you think? I just asked you to tell the story.

Okay! No more interruptions.

. . .

Well, as I was telling you, when they put me on that new medication, they said there would be side effects, but I never expected anything like what happened. *Hallucinations* wasn't a side effect they mentioned. I had come upstairs to bed, and I was sitting just like this, on the edge of the mattress, leaning over to take off my shoes and my pantyhose, and I looked over through the open door at the stairs. There was a little car on the top step, bright yellow. Even from this distance I could see that instead of wheels it had four little feet with five little toes each, five little toenails.

It made sense at the time, like how dreams make sense while you're dreaming them. But it wasn't a dream, and I thought, isn't that nice—the car must have lost its wheels somewhere, and it grew feet to replace them. It would never move as fast as it could with wheels—just imagine! But at least it could move a little. And sure enough, as I watched, the little car lifted its belly off the floor and began to strut along the top of the step until it reached the wall. And while this happened, another car appeared, this time bright red, behind it, with four little feet, just the same. And then a blue car, and then a green, and finally I was quick enough to see that they were being placed there by a hand, that there was someone sitting below on the stairs hiding from me, putting the cars up on the step.

There they all were, quiet and waiting: little toy cars, on the top of the step, lined up like they were in a traffic jam.

When the hand had finished, and the top step was full, I stood and went over to the stairs, but there was no one there. The stairs were empty. Eventually I went back to bed and to sleep and when I woke in the morning the little cars were gone.

See, this is the problem, Colleen interjects. This is why you worry me. You tell it so seriously, like it really happened.

It did really happen. Only I know now that it only really happened in my head.

Colleen exhales through her lips.

Oh, come on. There's some sound logic in that. Anyway, that isn't quite the end. I can't say for sure who was putting the little cars on the step, but I have a pretty good guess.

And what's that?

Well, when I stood up to find out who it was, something else was empty besides the stairs. One of the pictures on the stairwell wall. The small one, right in the middle—the one you hate so much. Like someone had stolen the photograph right out of the frame.

So you think—

—I don't think any of this, not seriously, you know that.

But in the realm of the story, the hallucination—

Sure, in the realm of the story.

That picture—

Yes.

. . .

What? What's that face for?

I'm putting you in a home for sure now.

Of course you are.

First thing tomorrow morning.

I'll be waiting.

Pack your things.

Sell them—you need the money.

Mom!

You started it.

And now I'll end it. It's time you got some sleep.

Colleen pulls the blankets up over her mother, who has leaned back against the pillows. Her cotton nightgown is a soft wall against the thinness of her legs. She blinks and smiles and turns her face aside.

Body [1½]

Ultimately, looking at the photograph and all of the sketches, she felt flattered to be segmented so articulately.

Face [2]

Colleen turns off the light and walks out of the bedroom and halfway down the stairs. She looks at the photograph on the stairwell wall, the small one, right in the middle. (The one she hates so much.) She reaches up and traces with one fingertip the black-and-white outline of the girl's cheekbone and jawline in the photograph, blurred with time. She's always had trouble looking at this image, always wondered why her mother kept it, but now she feels the sharp, beginning edge of fascination growing inside of her, a sense of intrigue like acid at the top of her stomach. She sees her own face [1] as her own face, and not a duplicate of this girl's [2]. Her mother was fifteen years old and dying. Colleen is middle-aged and has never been sick once, not in the real way that pinches at the edges of death. She looks back into the bedroom, up the stairs, and sees her mother's face turned sideways on the pillow, her hair spilling out like foam around her scalp, her neck skin sagging, melting into the cream of the sheets, her face in profile, the swell of the nose, the lips, the forehead, the dip of the eye sockets, the droop of the lids hanging upward over the eyes that look for a moment into the hallway light, a small glassy reflection there of yellow. Colleen blinks and, in the same dim slope of the hallway light sapping into the bedroom, she sees a girl in the bed—petite— the same girl from the stairwell photograph, the second dying folding into the first: looking keenly at Colleen, a small, glassy reflection there of yellow.

Colleen meets the gaze of this mirage, the patchy and fragmented girl. She meets the keen gaze briefly. The gaze keening. Cursory recognition. Then she goes downstairs and turns off the kitchen TV, which is obtrusive in the big house, yapping like static, like incomprehension, in the background of the silence of sleep.

As an elderly person being cared for by a younger generation, says Arthur, gesturing toward Husha and Nellie, I feel I should say something.

Husha nods, marking their place in her mother's book, just after the third story, "Mouth," and then flipping it closed. Sure, she says, of course. What would you like to say?

Arthur shrugs. He relaxes back into his chair, body slack, one knee rising to cross over the other. He's wearing a worn gray pullover sweater, emblazoned with the large black letters "UWO" on the front, that seems to swallow him up, his thin frame disappearing into the sweater's fabric. I don't know, he says. I just feel that I *should* say something.

Nellie laughs, a meteoric, unexpected sound that ricochets around the furniture and walls. Arthur and Husha raise their eyebrows simultaneously, the genetic makeup of their faces suddenly matching, and Nellie claps a hand over her mouth, breaking the sound of her laughter off at its source.

Sorry, she says. I've just never heard you make a joke before. That was a joke, wasn't it?

Arthur lifts a hand and runs his fingers through the sparse white tangle of hair on his head. My attempt at one, at least, he says. He shifts his old bones against the chair cushions and looks at the window across the room. Their reflections sit watery inside of the glass, Nellie in her usual place on the couch, leaning away from him, and Husha down on the floor by his feet. Both Nellie's and Husha's limbs are twisted into incomprehensible positions—Husha with her legs crossed and tucked beneath her, and Nellie with her knees pulled up under her chin—lithe, flexible, joints jutting at odd angles like those of a baby deer. The window reflection contorts them further, turning their bodies liquid and alien, bizarre as a Picasso painting.

Arthur wouldn't say he's envious of their youth—he remembers that phase of his life as exhausting and uncertain, the length and ardor of his PhD, the detached and hollow span of time before he met Sonia. More significantly, to be envious of their youth would be to discount his present experience, the gradual and yet rapid process of growing old, the way his body and mind seem to slope toward an ever-narrowing funnel, the way his thoughts seem to drag downward, hanging irretrievable somewhere near the bottom of his jaw instead of the top of his head. He's tired in old age, sure—always tired and always in some kind of discomfort, living in a pillowed and slippery chaos, but he finds something agreeable and satisfying, something worthwhile, at least, in his current state of being. Like reaching your bed after a long day of running marathons. Like lifting, finally, your swollen feet from the floor.

He may have made Nellie laugh, but he isn't certain of what drove him to it, isn't comfortable with the insecurities that crowded his throat after Husha finished reading his daughter's story. In retrospect, he finds he doesn't approve of the way Colleen's mother was presented, an apparently exemplary elderly person. Must I be witty and sharp, Arthur wonders, to be listened to? Must I be self-reflective, recognize and expose my own shortcomings, my body's malfunctions, as the woman in the story cheerfully examines her own hallucinations? Is there no room for authentic vulnerability, for admissions of terror or devastation? Most disturbingly—like the woman in the story—must I always be a metaphor for death? A reminder to the young that life is transient? Sickness personified—am I simply some literary device?

Arthur frowns, brows crunching together. He becomes aware that Husha and Nellie are watching him.

Did I say something? he asks, truthfully unable to remember.

No, says Husha, but you looked like you might.

Well, says Arthur. He clears his throat. He feels the night hanging over him, that darkness outside the window. Well, in all seriousness, there's something touching to it—and something disappointing.

To the story? asks Nellie.

Mm, grunts Arthur. Yes.

Go on, says Husha.

(Why must you validate yourself through analysis, exposition? wonders Arthur, deep inside his head. Why must you hold their attention?)

The theme of caring, he says aloud, of taking care of someone, is touching—affecting. But I don't think the story captures the scope of the act. Which is disappointing.

The scope of the act of caring?

Yes. He clears his throat again, trying to disperse a clump of dryness that has settled just behind his Adam's apple. He feels as if he's apologizing to Husha and Nellie, although this wasn't his intention. He thinks of Husha stirring a pot of soup on the kitchen stove, hauling laundry down the hallway, Nellie pulling grocery bags from the back of the car. The story neglects the boredom inherent in the act, he says. He pauses. And the likelihood of selfishness.

Husha unfolds her feet from beneath her and sits back with her hands on the carpet, leaning into her wrists. I understand what you mean by boredom, she says, pinching a smile off at her lips. But selfishness? Isn't it the opposite?

Taking care of someone else can be dishonest, says Arthur. Masked narcissism. Hypocrisy.

Nellie is nodding slowly on the couch. No such thing as altruism, she murmurs.

What? says Husha.

Hm? says Nellie, coming out of her daze.

Perhaps a story would serve as a better explanation, says Arthur. He places the balls of his feet on the floor and begins to rock his chair back and forth. He tents his fingers in front of his chest. The lamplight is low. As a lecturer, storytelling was half his profession, and he eases into the role like pulling on old, familiar clothes.

Yes! says Nellie. A story. An addition to the collection.

It's a true story, says Arthur. But it's not mine.

Husha exhales. All right, she says. We're listening. Now, out with it.

* * * *

THE STORY belongs to a friend of mine, a woman who was once a colleague at the university. I suppose the story *belonged* to her because she died a couple of years ago—or at least that's what I assume because she stopped sending me Christmas cards. Her name was Elizabeth, but everyone called her El. She was about five years older than me and often bragged that she was the first woman ever, in history—that's how she said it—*The first woman ever, in history, to graduate from the University of Toronto with a PhD in plant pathology.* She was fairly certain that statistic went beyond the University of Toronto, too. Anyway, we met when I accepted my position at UWO. She was brilliant, diplomatic. She worked tirelessly. She was also unmarried for an unusual length of time, a fact which made our colleagues uncomfortable when speaking with her. Perhaps it's needless to say she was the only woman in the department.

But you weren't uncomfortable speaking with her? cuts in Nellie, eyes gleaming. From her expression, Husha can tell that she's ready for the woman, Elizabeth, to fly off in a plane and proclaim herself Amelia Earhart.

Arthur hums at the back of his throat, thinking. I suppose—he says finally. I suppose I sometimes thought about the fact that she was unmarried. But my mother had lived alone for so long and so successfully after my father died that it wasn't a foreign circumstance. But now, El wasn't a widow, and she didn't have children, which made her slightly more—what's the word?

Dangerous, says Nellie.

Husha rolls her eyes.

I was going to say *problematic*—for that time, at least. Now, says Arthur, scowling, looking over at Nellie, wipe that smile off your face. I was deeply involved with your grandmother, he says, nodding at Husha, and we would soon be married.

Even better, Nellie mutters mischievously.

Nellie! says Husha. She gives her a look of warning across the coffee table. Nellie lifts her hands, ducking her head in submission.

Arthur watches the exchange. He waits. Okay, he says, once again steepling his fingers. Maybe it's worth clearing the air by saying this isn't a love story, not of any kind.

Nellie huffs loudly and sinks back against the couch.

A couple of years after working together, continues Arthur, I discovered that El had access to a family farm on the outskirts of London, which she would visit to retrieve certain plant samples. At the time, I was beginning work on a book on blue mold, so I asked her if I could tag along to look for affected plants in the area. She agreed, but only if I could find my own transportation to and from the farm.

Of course I assumed this stipulation had to do with her status as an unmarried woman and her unwillingness to be spotted in a vehicle alone with one of her colleagues, on their way to a mostly deserted farm—her uncles occasionally stopped in to tend the land—for an undetermined amount of time. It was a flawed presumption on my part because she never much cared for those types of things, public image and the like—you should have seen her thumping around the farm fields in her rubber boots, hair flying. Most of the time, I think she forgot I was there at all. She would be at the farm before I arrived and would stay who knows how long after I left. I simply thought she was dedicated to her work. It wasn't until my car broke down that I learned a little of what was going on.

Even with my vehicle out of commission for what my mechanic said might be more than a week, she refused to drive me to the farm. I was selfish and a little rude, I expect, and kept trying to persuade her until she had had enough and started yelling. And then I started yelling at *her* about how anyone worth her consideration wouldn't think twice of her being alone in a car with her colleague. She was obviously confused. Then she came to understand my thinking and decided she should explain.

Like I said, this is her story, not mine, and it goes like this:

When she was very young, El lived on that same farm with her parents and her little brother. Her parents owned cattle and grew corn, and her father sold preserves at local farmers' markets on the weekends. Theirs was a highly traditional household, and while her father worked on the field, her mother worked in and around the house. Everyone was always busy, and her mother was regularly sick. Frequently, her mother would go to town for doctor's visits, and El would be in charge of looking after her little brother, whose name was Paul. She was nine years old. Paul was six.

Once they finished their chores, El and Paul were free to go where they pleased. They sometimes visited the cows in the barn and dared each other to squeeze their udders, or climbed high up into the rafters to try and touch the gaps in the ceiling—this is how El described it—where light spilled through. Sometimes they went into the outhouse at the edge of the garden and practiced how long they could hold their breath inside. Sometimes they went into the forest and climbed trees or worked on a fort they were building with stray logs and pine branches. Or sometimes, when in season, they collected berries by the creek.

They called them river berries, although El said in retrospect they must have been gooseberries: peachy-red in color, sometimes tart, making their stomachs hurt if they ate too many of them. Their mother liked to mash the berries into jams. El and Paul would collect them for her, especially if she wasn't feeling well, and, when the sun grew hot midafternoon, they would take breaks from berry-picking to dip into the shallow end of the creek. It was a rule that Paul couldn't go in the water when El wasn't around because he wasn't a great swimmer—again, he was only six years old.

But rules are meant to be broken, and El and Paul had broken many rules together. One day, when El grew tired of Paul—apparently he was a particular menace that day, whining about his sore feet—and told him to stay by the river berries while she went to gather some wood for their fort, and yelled at him to leave her alone when he tried to follow her, he went into the creek—out of spite or boredom, El never found out—and drowned.

Naturally everyone was upset and distraught, as with all accidents of that sort, but it was a little different for El, who had not only been the one to leave him alone but was also the one to find him and drag him from the water. She said he must have been eating river berries before he went in, that his cheeks and hands were stained peachy-red.

Arthur pauses, finding his words. He looks at Husha and Nellie, who have finally stopped fidgeting in their seats, running fingers through their hair, or picking at fluffs on their clothes, who now sit still and attentive.

I told you, says Arthur, that this isn't any kind of love story.

El, he continues, being nine years old, didn't know what to do with her trauma. Her parents weren't exactly equipped to help, either, especially not her mother, who was increasingly indisposed. So, after the funeral, El's parents shut the door to Paul's bedroom and everything started up again, seamlessly, the rhythm of the day marching on, her mother milking the cows, cleaning the house, mending clothes, preparing dinner, and her father heading out to the fields. El, as we might expect, was unmoored. Not only had she lost her brother and playmate, but she had also lost her sense of duty and responsibility: she had nothing left to care for. Nothing to take care of.

Nellie makes a small noise on the couch, like a cough cut in half, a wet click deep in her throat.

Arthur hesitates. Anything to add? he asks.

Hm? says Nellie, then shakes her head. No—nothing, she says quickly. Nothing.

All right. Well. So. What was El to do? She tried to mimic her parents and return to life as usual. She completed her chores in the morning, as usual. But in the afternoon the *usual* thing to do was go out and adventure and take care of Paul. And so, following this impulse, she went down to the creek where he died, and, before she realized what she was doing, was waist-deep in the water in the shallow end.

It was August and the water was warm. El told me that something about the slow regularity and consistency of the current felt good on her legs. It felt soothing in a way nothing else had since Paul died. It felt comforting, like stability. Cleansing. There was also something sacred in standing in the last physical space that Paul had inhabited while living. She said she could feel him there, as if he were watching her from just under the water's surface.

She began going to the creek every day and standing in the water. It became her ritual. Sometimes she cried, sometimes she talked to herself, talked to Paul, but mostly she just stood there and stared into the water. In the fall, when school started up again, she had to rearrange her schedule and began running off to the creek between the moment when the school bus dropped her off and her mother set the table for dinner. Finally curious about her daughter's disappearances, her mother followed her one day and saw her standing in the water. El still doesn't know what her mother thought of her, but she was chastised, sent to her room, and forbidden from going to the creek alone.

She kept going. She had to. She told me there was no question, that it had become as much a necessity as eating or breathing. She went at night, started sneaking out of the house. Cooler weather arrived along with the beginning of October, and the water was icy in the dark when she stepped into it. She did not hesitate, didn't relent. In the winter, when the creek had frozen over, she would scoot down to the edge and break the ice with her bootheels before taking the boots off and sticking her feet in the water.

This couldn't last, of course. El developed frostbite on her feet and had to go to the doctor. She admitted to her parents what she had done. The doctor suggested a change in scenery, so her mother rented a small house in the city and lived there with El. It was a temporary arrangement. Her father visited on the weekends. The family was falling apart—her father couldn't do both the farm work and take care of the house, and her mother had nothing to do in the city. Meanwhile, El had substituted the creek for a cold bathtub, which only just satisfied her compulsion. Eventually her father gave up and got a job in the city and moved in with El and her mother. They sold their animals but kept the farm as an investment property and let El's uncles, who had farmland nearby, rent and till the fields.

That's how, years later, when El began work at the university, the farm was available for her research. What she had to admit to me when she wouldn't give me a ride in and out of town was that she had never stopped going to the creek, not really. When she turned sixteen and got her driver's license, she would borrow her parents' car and go to the farm. She had been going once a week, at least, for her entire adult life. On the days when I came to gather plant samples, she would wait until I left before heading to the water.

I guess she assumed I would think she was crazy, but really I just felt sorry for her. After all the time that had passed since Paul died, she hated the creek. She couldn't feel Paul in the water anymore, could barely remember what he looked like. Worst of all, she was bored of her ritual. I remember her asking me, *Is this love? An act of love? Did I love him?* From an outside perspective, she appeared fiercely dedicated, like some sort of tragic hero. But she didn't feel anything. I know because she asked me once, *What does it mean if I feel nothing?* I think she was really asking, *What happens when our love becomes routine?* The truth was that, in the end, after enough time had gone by, it didn't bother her anymore that she had left her brother behind when it was her duty to care for him and came back to find him drowned. She was underwhelmed by the worst possible event in her life, and the most horrifying. She was unaffected, undismayed.

* * * *

HUSHA AND Nellie wait a moment to see if he will say anything more. The house seems to hunker down around them—it acquired, while Arthur was speaking, that deep, hollow silence that only arrives sometime after midnight, like behind every wall is a held breath.

So, Husha says at last, her voice an interruption to the serenity she sees on her grandfather's face. I guess we know your answer to that question—"Is this love?" You did say it wasn't a love story.

Mm, says Arthur. Mm-hm. He nods, his chin dipping lower each time it drops. His eyes begin to water, and his mouth opens in a slow, rubbery yawn. Perhaps my answer was different back then, he says, but now I'm cynical, old. Look at me—he raises a hand to wrap his fingers around another yawn. Can't even stay awake for my own story.

Without ceremony, as is his custom, hardly even a "g'night" mumbled under his breath, Arthur leans forward, heaves himself from the chair, and begins to shuffle his way around the couch and into the kitchen. Husha calls to him, a faltering sound, still surprised by his abrupt departures, and he tosses a hand behind him in a half wave as he moves down the hall.

His bedroom door clicks as it closes.

Well, Nellie exhales, turning sideways and extending her legs down the length of the couch. That was interesting.

What do you mean? asks Husha. She stands and stretches, reaching her hands over her head. Her shirt lifts and reveals her pale stomach, the cleft of skin retreating beneath her rib cage.

Nellie lays the back of one hand against her closed eyes. The only reason I didn't say anything while he was talking, says Nellie, dropping her voice in case Arthur hasn't yet settled into sleep, is because I knew you would yell at me afterward if I did.

Husha laughs. I don't yell at you, she says.

Okay, your version of yelling, then. You would speak to me sternly and tell me how I've misbehaved.

Husha drops her arms and shrugs. She steps around the coffee table, lifts Nellie's feet, and positions herself beneath them, Nellie's heels in her lap, on the couch. Her hands cup and wander the dimples on either side of her Achilles' tendons.

How did you want to misbehave? Husha asks.

Nellie smirks. Don't start, she says, but nevertheless pushes her heels down between Husha's legs. Really, though, I wanted to tell him—and here her voice falls fully into whisper—that the story is complete bullshit. It's like a modern fairy tale teaching young women the dangers of independence.

Husha frowns. How so?

Well, think about it. The minute this Elizabeth chick loses her male counterpart, the person she has no choice but to take care of, she goes crazy and—sorry, that was a bit insensitive—she develops what could probably be deemed OCD and returns to the creek apparently forever, disguising it as "work." And—and—says Nellie, propping herself up on her elbows—I think the implication is, considering how many times your grandpa mentioned her marital status, that El's malady could be solved, or cured, or—whatever—if she would just find herself a husband already and start taking care of him instead of her dead brother.

Now, says Husha, that last bit might be a stretch.

Even so. Nellie flops back onto the armrest of the couch.

Hm, says Husha. She fiddles with Nellie's bare toes, stares forward into the dead fire. I didn't really see it that way, she says. She deliberates. Couldn't it also be a modern fairy tale teaching the dangers of becoming too invested in caring for another person? You know, getting too much out of it, basing too much in it, or making it your whole identity? Didn't my grandpa start the whole story off by saying care can be hypocritical—selfish?

Yeah, says Nellie, sure. And I get that. I don't really believe in altruism either. Everybody gets something out of helping another person, even if they don't want to admit it. *Especially* if they don't want to admit it. But in that story, it just feels too convenient. Like—thanks for all of your unpaid labor, women and girls, as you take care of every man around you, but we know in the end that it's a selfish act and you're all doing it to give your life some purpose and boost your egos. I don't know, says Nellie. She throws up her hands. You can't win.

Husha nods. I think there is something to what he was saying at the end, though, she says. We don't really have a definition for true care. Does it count as care if it isn't altruistic? Is there such a thing as care if altruism is impossible? Like, I get that you can take care of someone and feel nothing, get no reward, but what is that, then? Compulsion? The result of a guilty conscience? Fear of what you might feel if you didn't take care of that person?

Even those involve some feeling, says Nellie. Guilt, fear. Not compulsion, though. That's more instinctual.

Not compulsion, no, says Husha. She purses her lips, squints. I guess my real question is—is there a difference between caring for someone and taking care of them? Does it equate to the same thing?

Nellie, off in her own world, is staring at the ceiling. She muses, I do like the way he phrased it: *Is this love? What does it mean if I feel nothing?*

Anne, Cassandra, and the Sleep House

ANNE

She wakes to the sound of rain and the sense that there is nothing she must do that day, nothing left incomplete, nothing that must be done. She wakes to the sound of rain (the sound) against the window beside the bed and sits in this sound longer than she might have on a day when she wakes to the sound of her husband's alarm clock, waking him for work. This alarm clock drags like the edge of ragged tin inside her ears. This alarm clock wakes Marcus, her husband, for work, to a day with strict boundaries, a start and a finish, the transition from sleep to consciousness rising sudden and definable, the house separated from the working world outside of it. This alarm clock wakes Anne brutally to a sense of hurry, to the baby who needs breakfast, the cat and its litterbox, the clutter she imagines already gathering on the kitchen counter—*enough*, she thinks. She shakes her head.

This morning, she wakes to the sound of rain and she sits in this sound.

SHE SITS (sleeps).

THINGS MUST BE DONE, she knows this. She knows there are things to do like in her head she knows there are scientific laws to gravity, but she doesn't feel this rush and hurry in her body like she feels gravity, which she feels deeply as her body sinks into the bed.

Contentment like gravity (this sound) in her body.

Could this sensation be—restfulness? Peace? Could it have come from sleep? She stares at the ceiling, listening to the rain at the window, and tries to remember the night: she feels she has come thundering through some dream she can't grab hold of. It slides back behind her eyeballs the moment she rolls them up to look. Dreams are wistful and slow, peculiar like all things make-believe. Anne loves dreams because she rarely has them anymore, and she rarely has them because she rarely sleeps.

* * * *

HER INSOMNIA began just after the wedding, after moving into this house. Both—the wedding and the house—happened on the same day. Her husband is Catholic, so there was no possibility of them moving into the house before their marriage. Anne supposed she agreed with the logic and ceremony of this decision. She understood ceremony and ritual; she believed in divinity. For these reasons, and because she had grown up with the Church, she supposed she was Catholic like her husband, although she really only went to mass anymore for the singing, the rhythmic, echoing organ, the tall, arching walls. There was something halting and worthwhile in the acoustics of the building. She supposed she was Catholic, but when she prayed she no longer used words. She was Catholic, she supposed, but her only remaining confession when she sat in the dark booth was, *I can no longer sleep.*

She was an insomniac. She had heard the word on the radio and felt it suited her in a way no other word ever had. Much better than *nocturnal*, which she had recently adopted into her vocabulary. *Nocturnal* felt inborn, whereas *insomnia* was an illness, and to be an insomniac was to be defined by this illness, was to have it slouch like a broken shoulder into every part of her day.

The house came with insomnia, or insomnia came with the house. She moved into this house the same day as her wedding. Had she mentioned that? The house was made up with furniture and photographs in preparation for their arrival the same way her face was made up with makeup, her hair curled back around her ears and her nails done in small, meticulous strokes by a woman who tried but could not remember Anne's name, the dress Anne had rented for the occasion creased but still appropriately white. The house was an unfamiliar but comfortable place to rest her body after such a long day, an unfamiliar shell much like the dress, much like the man she knew well but not in this context, a house and bed to rest in now without sin. Her body a body for Marcus to rest in.

Was it the wedding or the house? She couldn't sleep. She lay awake and listened to Marcus breathing, watching the dark, flat plane of the ceiling. It couldn't be the wedding, because she loved the wedding and had wanted it all her life. It was as she had pictured it. Her parents were very happy. Her mother cried. The church was regal, beautiful. Christmas was approaching and everything was strewn with lights. Her father was stoic: he approved. Her friends were giddy with the knowledge of her pending consummation. And her husband—the man, Marcus, who that day became her husband—commented afterward that it was a sophisticated ceremony, that everyone had done a good job, the flowers were placed expertly, the guests seemed to have a *nice time*. These were comments he knew she wanted to hear, because the reception took place in her parents' large basement, everyone trundling in out of the cold and piling their damp coats in the front hallway, potluck-style for food and the music coming from her brother's record player because the band they had convinced to play for cheap had dropped out at the last moment. And how generous, how thoughtful it was for Marcus to offer comments that he knew she wanted to hear. She felt so lucky, so at peace with him driving them home to their new house, still in her dress, so lucky that she felt stricken and numb as if there had been some mistake. As if her body had been swapped in for someone else's, an imposter in her own chosen union, as if they had forgotten the car keys two miles back but still, somehow, were driving.

How could anyone be so lucky?

She was lucky, certainly, to live in such a beautiful home (she couldn't sleep). After going through the open house with Marcus and her mother, she had wanted the house in a way she had never wanted anything before in her life—a feeling distinct from her desire for a wedding, for a marriage and family. This house felt heavier, like insistence, like inevitability. For starters, the front door was dark red. The front porch was small and white and wooden and creaked when she stepped onto it. The front hallway was narrow and full of mirrors. There was hardly space to put her boots by the door. There was hardly room for thinking beneath the low-hanging chandelier in the dining room. The fireplace in the living room was jammed with different shapes and colors of stone, and the kitchen tiles were tiny and so polished that when she bent down, she saw her eye reflected back at her. The bathroom had a claw-foot tub. The bedroom had a large window looking out onto the yard. A forest leaned over the fence line. The cellar smelled like wintertime and wet stone.

Marcus wandered the house, probing closets and cupboards, touching doorframes.

It has a stately quality to it, doesn't it? he said.

Does it? asked Anne. It seemed too masculine a descriptor. To her, the house felt fertile and soft. In the cellar, in a crack in the cement wall, she had discovered a cluster of mushrooms growing.

Be careful what you call your home, said Anne's mother, making Marcus roll his eyes. After he had left the room, she said, leaning into her daughter, I'm serious. You must treat it with respect. A house is a woman's most intimate companion, and, as we know with all intimacies, it's a relationship that can turn nasty very quickly.

Anne sighed. She drew her finger along the curve of a metal doorknob. She muttered, Next you'll be telling me you think the place is haunted.

Her mother laughed. Nothing so monstrous, she said.

The house was out of their price range—$50,000—but her mother was feeling sentimental about her only daughter leaving

Erica McKeen

home and decided to help with the down payment. The mortgage payments would be more than they anticipated, but they could make it work with Marcus's reasonable teaching salary. Anne could always work, too, if it were necessary. She had gone to college for hairdressing and could turn the kitchen into a makeshift salon. She assumed it would take a while to start a family, and working might be a good way to pass that time.

Anne's assumptions were wrong. She got pregnant, and faster than she thought was possible. But by then she was so tired she wasn't fully certain how much time had passed. It was January when she missed her period, so that meant it had been a month, at least, since the wedding. That first night in the house, she reasoned, must have been the moment of conception.

She averaged three hours of rest a night, during which she wasn't sure if she became fully unconscious. Through the large bedroom window and in thick moonlight, the backyard took on a strange glow. A creamy, alien landscape. She often walked outside and looked over the back fence into the trees. The forest behind their house was full of owls. She listened to the birds' soft hooting in the dark patterns of bark and leaves. Anne sat on the couch sometimes and counted the number of stones in the fireplace. She read books that she didn't remember the next morning. They lay open (like a woman's legs) in her lap. Her stomach grew larger. She cleaned baseboards. She was pregnant and had swollen legs. In the cellar, she touched the walls and found that they were wet.

Her mother came for tea in the mornings.

Your garden is blooming out front, she said.

Anne didn't remember planting the tulip bulbs that she saw splitting open there in the dirt.

Would you look at those toes, said Marcus, after Anne gave birth in a stupor to their first child. He cupped one small foot in his hand. The toes were smaller than marbles, pink and squirming. Anne was tired. She had been in labor for nineteen hours and felt finally like she might fall asleep.

She didn't sleep. She stayed awake and felt the ripeness between her legs swell and envelop her body like a fluid balloon. The baby found her breast and began to suck and relieve tension in her chest that she didn't know she had been holding. But also in this suckling came a release of tough muscle, the components of herself, a loosening of bone.

She wanted to go back to her house and lie on the carpet on the floor.

The hospital was dull brown with high ceilings, full of noises.

Later, her husband took the baby screaming from the room.

Later, she was home again with the baby screaming in her lap. She still felt lucky, and increasingly necessary to the lives happening around her. These thoughts smoothed the knotted lobes of her brain. She put the baby away in the crib like sliding a sock into a drawer and filled a bucket, scalding, to scrub the kitchen floor.

CASSANDRA

The rain is coming down is coming down in slow, persistent sheets, a rolling patter at the window and dappling the trees, when Cassandra wakes and tries to explain to her mother, who has come to get her ready for school, and her brother, too, who is staring at her from his bed across the room, that she doesn't feel right in the confines of her body, that she's expanding beyond the limits of her skeleton. She can't say it in these words—she's only twelve years old—but she wants to say that the feeling has something to do with the rain, a compression and release, some fading electricity in the air. The rain smells deep and cosmic like mud, like the slick armpit of a toad or the dewy, spongy underside of a mushroom cap. The rain outside the window is minuscule in each droplet, but also immense. The sky is opening up.

(Like a woman's legs opening for birth.)

As she looks at her mother and brother, Cassandra blinks and blushes, struggling to find suitable words and remembering suddenly a glimpse of her recent dream, the dream that fades quickly behind her eyes.

(Like a woman's legs opening for—breath.)

I'm floating, Cassandra manages to say. I think I'll float through the ceiling.

* * * *

CASSANDRA MOVED into the house four months after her parents' divorce. It was a house her mother said they could only afford—$400,000—because of the incoming alimony checks. Her mom said they needed a fresh start, that there were too many memories lodged in the cracks between the floorboards at their old house, that she could smell Cassandra's father on doormats and in the folds of curtains. Cassandra didn't understand the problem—her father smelled warmly of salt and hair gel, of the books he read and the leather of the seats in his car. She had lived in the same house her entire life. It was a comfortable place to live, like a good pair of jeans, like assimilation, like routine.

Moving houses meant moving schools and neighborhoods, so she was far from her friends when, on her first night in the new house, she got her period. In the unfamiliar bathroom with its strange, claw-foot tub, she pulled down her pants to use the toilet and found a brown smudge in her underwear. The white toilet paper came up stained. Cassandra ran to the family computer, which her brother had set up in the living room, signed into her email account, and messaged her friends. She was the last of them to start bleeding. By the time she went to her mom, who was watching TV in her bedroom, a deep, hurtling pain had filled her lower abdomen. Her mother gave her pads and showed her how to clean herself.

It's important to shower regularly, her mother said. She paused. So you don't develop a smell.

Instead of a smell, Cassandra quickly developed an aversion to herself. She wanted to take her mother's hand-held mirror and inspect the folds of skin between her legs, which felt hot and wounded, with the same impulse that leads a person to stick their fingers in an electrical outlet. Paradoxically, simultaneously, she wanted to never look at or think of her body again. Before bed, she hid her used pad in a cocoon of toilet paper and then deep within the garbage can. She imagined she could smell the blood wafting up to meet her nostrils, a dark, humid scent, like baking mold.

That first night in the house—was it the house or her menstruation?—she couldn't sleep. Her brother, hair tousled, lay snoring in the bed across the room. She watched moving shadows from the window lick the ceiling. The next day, on her way to and at school, empty-headed and dizzy, nervous about being a newcomer, she saw women on the street, in cars, her teachers and the girls in her classes, and imagined them bleeding, liquid heat between their legs. She imagined the lump of flesh between their legs; she smelled pennies in her nose. She was exhausted and sweaty under her arms, wanted to go home and wash the back of her tongue with hand soap.

Cassandra didn't sleep the following night, or the night after that. Her mother and brother didn't know. Cassandra was quiet when she had to be, and full of whispers deep inside her throat. *Insomnia*—it was something she thought only happened in movies. But here she was, cemented into reality, and she couldn't sleep. Was it the house or was it her body? Could she make such a distinction? She didn't believe in haunted houses, nothing as monstrous as that, but she understood now what her mother had associated with their previous home, how thoughts could stick to walls and fester. Start to grow.

She wandered (the house wandered her) through the house. It was old and held up by worn-looking plaster, corners hiked into the roof like hunched shoulders. The front door was old red, deep maroon that her mother wanted to paint cream white for a more modern touch. But the house could never be modern and had creaking floorboards, stones stuffed into the structure of its fireplace like braceless teeth. Her mother discovered asbestos in the cellar, in the paint covering the pipes, and forbade Cassandra from going down. The stairs to the cellar were long and wooden with a splintered railing. Cassandra went down at night (she couldn't sleep) and stared at the old washing machine, at the rust stains carving saw-toothed, brown triangles into the white ceramic. And what a kitchen, with its small, cracked tiles. And what a chandelier in the dining room, always dusty. She loved the house like she had never loved anything before in her life. In her dreams (if she dreamt), she shrunk the house to the size of her body and put her arms around it, put her hands inside of it, her fingers in the windows.

Shutters opening, she heard them moaning.

The house had been lived in by an old woman who recently died. It was sold by her children who had grown up there. They didn't care much for the house, but their mother had loved it—stayed with it long after their father died—and so they were sad to see it go. Cassandra was with her mother at the open house, looking out the large bedroom window while listening to the adults talk. Yes, they were sad to see the house go. See it go where? Cassandra wondered. She could feel that this house would never leave, that it would sit inside the earth like it sat inside people. The house sat inside her belly like warm soup. It pulled a yearning up inside of her like the gulp before crying or the urge in her bladder to pee.

Cassandra found mushrooms growing down in the cellar, slim, white-capped cones of rubber sticking out from a crack in the wall. The mushrooms reminded her of the fungus her mother had warned her might spore throughout her own body—yeast. Like the ingredient that rises bread. The cellar smelled like bread left underwater. It was night and she had wandered downstairs. The cement walls, under her fingertips, were wet.

Cassandra, Cassandra—her mother was shaking her—*wake up. Why won't you open your eyes?*

But her eyes were already open. She could see her mother

shaking her as she reclined on the couch. She was out under the moon and had the sounds of owls in her hair. Her feet were leading her down the cellar stairs, her feet moving in front of her.

The house carried her—away from thoughtlessness, away from sleep.

THE SLEEP HOUSE

In the dream, in her first real sleep in months, Anne walks through the front hallway and ignores her reflection. She moves into the kitchen and finds a bucket of water. She pulls it down from the counter and begins scrubbing the floor. Her back aches. Her strokes are rhythmic and circular, domestic ritual. Somewhere behind her head, she sees a girl pass through the kitchen doorway and head toward the cellar stairs.

In the dream, in her first real sleep in months, Cassandra passes through the kitchen doorway and sees a woman bent over a bucket of water, scrubbing and scrubbing and scrubbing the floor. Cassandra looks down and sees that she is bleeding. Her jeans are soaked an old red, maroon. Heat pulses down her legs, and she can feel the house throbbing around her like a heart. Her hand reaches for the cellar door.

In the dream, Anne looks up. The girl is going down is going down the cellar stairs. A smell leaks up through the open doorway. Musty, unwashed, the cellar has developed a smell.

In the dream, the blood is going down is going down and pooling in Cassandra's socks. She leaves footprints as she walks. Behind her, the woman bends her neck into the doorway and watches her descend.

Anne looks down and sees that she is dressed all in white.

Her hands are old, full of wrinkles. She has been scrubbing until her fingers burn.

She stands, gathers her long wedding dress in her hands—gathers the dress that she rented for the wedding, the dress that other women wore before her, wore after—and heads down the stairs.

Cassandra, then Anne, finds the down-low damp of the cellar floor. The earth underneath vibrates. The house holds urgency in its hulking mass. An expectant tremble, a murmur: must.

This shake, ache, this trembling. The cellar descending inward. And outward (they are sleeping). She is sleeping she is screaming, mouth open. The house screams into the ache between Anne and Cassandra's legs. If she could, she would straddle this mold, the damp, the dreaming and awake, the blood, she remembers the bleeding, the first bleeding, something like wet cement buckling between attic rafters, shifting the foundation. The stretch in the soles of her feet. Ah, ah, ah. She is walking down the stairs and sliding her fingers—ah

—along the banister. Swallowing the house's must in mouthfuls. The smell of the house like sawdust, chunks of rooftop, paper drywall down her throat. The must hooking into her nostrils. The must, the must. The must that keeps her waking, keeps her awake. She sits on the floor and fits her hand into the mushroom-filled crack in the wall.

Her knuckles scrape cement.

Her fingers grip.

The house imperceptibly latches.

And shakes.

Ah.

She feels another woman sitting there inside of her. She is young and she is old. She is mopping floors. She is holding a baby inside of her, heavy against her hips. She is growing breasts, hips widening. She is inside of her(self), inside this house. She opens up and draws the house in closer, leans back, clenches, and wails. Her fingers are bloody (ragged cement) inside her body, ragged wailing.

The must, the must like luxury, release.

* * * *

SHE WAKES.

The rain is falling soft outside the window. (Who slides away with careful hands?)

Her hands are mopping—tears from her face. She has never felt so hollow and sinks deep into the mattress. She might float. In her body is the sense that she should sleep, that she *can* sleep. That there is nothing to be done today, nothing left half-finished, nothing more for her to do.

IN THE EVENING, when they're ready to begin their reading, Husha and Nellie wonder where Arthur could be. He isn't in his chair in the living room—isn't in the kitchen, clawing through the fridge, searching for something sweet to round off dinner, or shuffling in patient privacy behind the closed bathroom door. When Husha goes to check, she can't find him in his bedroom, the laundry room, the garden outside.

Maybe he's down by the lake, offers Nellie.

Grandpa! calls Husha through the window screen above the kitchen sink.

They listen for his muffled reply. Husha finds him down in the cellar, a place she only rarely goes, dark wooden winding stairs, packed dirt floor, a tiny space Arthur built—hollowed out—with his own hands. Dust and junk and mold.

Grandpa, says Husha, what are you doing down here?

Arthur, crouched in the corner, looks down at his wrinkled palms. They're covered in a gray film of dust. Open boxes gape upward around him. A single, bare lightbulb illuminates the shape and texture of his scalp.

Looking for something, Arthur mumbles. Husha watches his knees trembling delicately, like a flame licking air, beneath his pant legs. Can't remember what.

Come here, says Husha. She beckons him, moves forward through the dirt, in her socks, to take his arm. Come here, come on, let's go upstairs.

Erica McKeen

* * * *

THE NEXT MORNING, after she showers, her hair damp around her neck and shoulders, Husha finds Arthur in the cellar again.

He's still in his pajamas—loose gray pants and a button-up navy shirt, long-sleeved—and his hair is tousled, uncombed. He doesn't wear shoes or socks, not even his slippers, and because of the way he kneels on the floor, almost on all fours, one arm slung around a large cardboard box and his heels tilted upward, she can see the nearly opaque layer of dirt coating the soles of his feet. The cardboard box is open and he's peering in, his face moving from side to side as if pushing invisible objects around with his nose.

Grandpa, says Husha from where she stands at the bottom of the staircase.

He flinches, his shoulders jumping up toward his ears, but doesn't turn to look at her.

You can help me bring it upstairs, he says, but you can't look inside.

He takes weight off his hand, leaning back on his knees and ankles, and begins to close the box flaps.

The cellar smells like sawdust and old paint. The air feels warm and heavy in Husha's nose and throat when she breathes in. As she descends the last step and moves across the cellar floor, ducking around the hanging lightbulb, Arthur closes the last flap of the box. Husha catches no glimpse of what is inside the box, only an angle of shadow before the flap falls into place.

She stands over Arthur and crosses her arms. The top of her head nearly brushes the exposed wooden framework of the ceiling; as a result, she dips her chin out of necessity, not in

136

an attempt to patronize. Regardless of her intentions, Arthur looks up at her like a child, stubborn and determined, defensive, a crease deepening between his eyebrows and his left arm still looped protectively around the box.

What is it? asks Husha. What's inside?

None of your concern, says Arthur. He leans back further into his ankles and tenses his forearms as if hoping to push off the floor and launch himself into a standing position, then thinks better of it. The hair along his forehead releases a drop of sweat that trails a wet line down his right temple and along the ill-defined curve of his jaw. Husha wonders how long he's been in the cellar, how long he's been awake. Dimly, like an alarm clock sounding, she hears the ring of the cicadas starting up outside.

Husha sighs.

She says, You'll be hard-pressed to enlist my help without telling me what's in that box.

Arthur scowls. Husha expects a snide remark, something about her increasing tendency to take advantage of his old age or her disrespect for his privacy, but he says nothing of the kind. He says nothing at all. He breathes in deeply through his nostrils. Again his forearms tense, and Husha thinks his muscles might be spasming, sees him fully for how small, how bent and tired he is, even this early in the morning. She wants to step forward and help him up but knows that he would be angry with her, frustrated and reclusive as he already is in this moment, closed off. Already she's angry with herself for finding him pitiable, for the way he has so unthinkingly presented himself as pitiable. She doesn't want his anger as well as her own.

Husha reaches up to squeeze the wet ends of her hair. Moisture slips into and across the palm of her hand. I won't look inside, she says, relenting a little, yielding, a little.

Arthur shakes his head slowly from side to side, once, twice, but he rotates his body and holds out his hand for her assistance.

None of your concern, he says again. Nothing to worry you. Just some of your mother's old things.

* * * *

HE WON'T tell her what's in the box, but he also refuses to leave it in the cellar. It's clunky and awkward and difficult to get up the narrow stairs. Once Husha successfully heaves the box through the kitchen, pausing only momentarily with the edge of it against the counter in order to readjust her grip, and then down the hallway and into Arthur's bedroom, placing it roughly on the floor by the window, Arthur sits on the end of his bed and begins talking, apparently having found his voice after leaving the dark, quiet swell of the cellar. You should see the other things down there, he says. The other things in the other boxes. Cleaning supplies and toolboxes and extra plastic bags, shovels for the wintertime, old bicycles, emergency supplies for a blackout: flashlights, candles. All utilitarian. Some purpose. He shuffles one foot out from under him and nudges the box with his toe. I got to thinking about this box and how it doesn't belong. I got to thinking about it down there and I couldn't stop thinking about it. I put it down there years and years ago after your mom stopped coming here during the summer. I'd forgotten that it existed. I'd prefer, he tilts his face up toward Husha, if you didn't look inside.

Husha, leaning against the wall, hands slinking down into her pockets, facing him, wants to ask, Why? But she knows it would be a useless question—she can see the answer already curled up in his expression: *I'd prefer if you left this portion of your mother's memory to me.*

She wants to ask why, but instead she asks for some hint, some idea of what's in the box. Give me a clue, she says. Maybe he can tell her how old her mother was when the things inside the box belonged to her. Maybe he can tell her more about why he put it in the cellar. Arthur shuffles his foot back underneath his knee, tucks his heel against the bedpost. He ignores her question but begins talking again, his pupils skittering away across his eyeballs. He scoops memories seemingly at random out of his mind. At first, Husha is confused, lost in the tangle of his line of thinking, but then she realizes he must be offering these memories in lieu of the objects in the box. Even here, she's wrong; she misunderstands. At this moment her grandfather's world is insular and does not expand to embrace her feelings or demands. He mumbles about her mother down by the lake making sand castles in the reeds, whispering, "It's a forest, can't you see? The grass is high over their heads." She must have believed, Arthur explains, that small people lived in her castle, existing somewhere like bubbles under the sand. He mumbles about her mother drawing pictures on the floor with crayon, a wide swath of paper that she soon forgot and cast aside, crayon mapping the floorboards instead, from the kitchen to the living room, spirals and scribbles, the occasional eyeball or the shape of a thick-fingered hand emerging from the mess, nothing wholly discernible. He mumbles about her mother napping on his wife's, Husha's grandmother's, chest. In the late afternoon, a rocking chair, a discarded book tented nearby on a table, sunlight on her kneecaps, the suck of dense summer air in his nose as he wandered into this scene, the slow mewl of their breath as they slept.

Husha's bottom lip is stuck between her teeth, and she can feel her shoulder blades where they pinch against the wall. In the pause, she doesn't speak, doesn't dare.

The width and length of her mother's feet and toes in childhood. When a son or daughter dies, Arthur says—and now she sees that he clutches the edge of the bedspread tightly—why do we remember them always as children? Is it because they are their most vulnerable then, and it's terrible we couldn't protect them as we promised, as we were meant to? I feel I can trace your mother's death back to the beginning. But in the same moment I feel I shouldn't. It would comfort me to find purpose, make some meaning, a narrative, claim utility, but there would also be a cheapening of her life and herself as a person by drawing such a definitive timeline. I don't think her leaving us was meant to be. I don't think the stars aligned. I don't think it was fate's doing. But I can still see her making soap bubbles in the bathtub, I can still feel her hooked up small and warm in my arms. Without giving it shape or meaning, I still find it huge, this dying, catastrophic. So huge it becomes incomprehensible, like wind, a hurricane pulling up and down inside my head.

Husha unclasps her lip from her teeth. Please can I see what's in the box, she asks, even as she hates herself for asking.

Arthur crimps his fingers tighter against the bedspread.

So huge it becomes insensible, he says.

* * * *

HUSHA WANTS MORE, wants all of her grandfather's stories, every detail of her mother as a child and teenager, the history of her life from the beginning. She has so many questions—they get stuck in her throat like a piece of clay that she has swallowed. Sometimes, when she, Nellie, and Arthur sit and settle into the living room before reading, Husha has to push her tongue against the back of her teeth to keep from speaking, to keep from hounding her grandpa: What was my mother's first word as a baby? When did she begin to crawl? What were her childhood birthday parties like, did she have many friends? What was she scared of? What were her bad habits, her injuries and adventures, what dreams did she have, did any come true?

Sometimes Husha has to push two knuckles into her mouth and bite down, hard, in order to keep the questions inside of her. Sometimes Nellie notices and, without knowing the genesis of Husha's anxiety, reaches over and cups her bent elbow in her hand. *Easy*, she says with her eyes. *Take it easy.*

Sometimes when the three of them sit and read together, Husha imagines them sitting on the ceiling. This image grants visual clarity and justification to her persistent and growing feeling of disorientation as they read her mother's book. They are on the ceiling, unconcerned, cross-legged. Because they are on the ceiling, the rest of the world is upside down—the room, with its couch and chair and lamps and rug, hangs the wrong way, according to gravity. The candle flame on the coffee table flickers downward. The wine clings inexplicably to the glasses. The three of them sit together, their necks bent toward the book between them. They won't look up (or down). Why won't they look up (or down)? Husha is reading and her voice grows thick around certain consonants, as if with mucus or phlegm. At times she's so angry that she can't hear herself speaking as she reads. So angry with her mother for all the things she didn't tell her, for the regimented methods she used to keep herself distant. And now Husha's anger transfers to her grandpa, who refuses to share his stories. He occasionally relents when she asks for more, but generally he withdraws, his lips puckering and hardening into a straight line. In those moments, have his thoughts drifted and become indecipherable to him, or does he think she shouldn't know?

None of your concern.

Does he sense and shrink away from her desperation? Does he believe she will be too affected? How can he, at the end of his own life when none of it should matter, be so selfish? How can it help, what could it mean, to take these memories with him when he dies?

Husha has the awareness to realize, at least, that he wants the same from her—a whole host of memories, a crowd of ghosts from Husha's past, adorned with the face of her mother, that would duck in to swallow him, possess him like demons. He wants stories from that life he cannot fathom: the life of a child, to be taken care of by Husha's mother, his daughter, instead of being the one taking care, the one worrying. And Husha cannot give her thoughts to him. She chokes on the memories that clot her mind.

The space between Husha and Arthur is dense with something like static electricity, a certain texture, a cloying film, in the air.

* * * *

As they read, Husha's mother hangs upside down between them, or right side up—whichever way is the opposite of them and how they sit with the book, heads bent and only every so often glancing up at each other. She hangs between them, usually silent, infrequently making small noises with her mouth closed, in the back of her throat, as if swallowing. Her hair hangs straight down with gravity and the muscles in her face also, due to gravity, are lifted and plump. Beneath (above) her eye sockets are little pouches of flesh. She isn't concerned about the orientation of her arms and they swing discordantly beside her ears. Her body between them is solid and insistent, despite them only every so often glancing up (and, even less frequently, noticing her there). The bottoms of her feet touch the ceiling and she rotates slowly, staring at each of them in turn.

In Transit

WHAT DOES IT MEAN to be a haunted place, or to be a haunted person?

Is it to live within a convergence of perspectives, to let alien contexts creep inside the cavities of your ears, under your eaves-troughs, the gutters meant to funnel the rain? Is it to loosen your shingles and floorboards and allow something unrecognized to pass through?

Is it to become your shadow and regard yourself walking?

Is it to find an unfamiliar family living in your home?

Is it to find a shred of fingernail in your salad at dinnertime that is not your own? To wonder how many of these not-your fingernails have tunneled through your body?

Is it to call a phone from a phone within a house using the same line, to answer yourself from a different room?

Is it to find something dead in the basement?

To find something dead in the garden in the backyard?

To find something dead in the bathtub with the water on?

Is it to fail at holding your story in by its borders, if there are such things as borders? Is it to be unsure of when your story in fact becomes another story, to be unsure of when to stop talking, whether or not you've already told this anecdote to a friend, where to place the quotation marks, to be unsure of when that voice now muffled outside the window is your own tongue moving at the back of your throat? Is it to look out a window at the dark night and see yourself reflected there, looking in?

* * * *

How DOES a house become a haunted house? Which shall we take as our example?

Should we consider this house, here, on the edge of Toronto, an old but stable house with two stories and a small attic space, a pinewood frame with tongue-and-groove construction and a concrete foundation? And if we do consider this house as an example, should we note that it is inconveniently situated where the city wishes to build a hospital, that it has been slated for demolition?

Did you know that not all houses slated for demolition are actually demolished? Did you know some are salvaged and transported to used-house lots and sold for cheap prices to people anxious to style themselves homeowners?

Did you know that at this time on the edges of Toronto there are many people anxious to style themselves homeowners?

Should we consider this company—Dave's Movers—as an example of one that has convinced the hospital construction crew to skip the pricy demolition and allow Dave of Dave's Movers himself to commandeer the project of uprooting and transporting our chosen home? And if we do consider this company as an example, should we note that Dave is not in the habit of paying respects to the foundation of the home, that he has bigger and more economically pressing matters to attend to, and that he uses a jackhammer to tunnel through the concrete base and insert support beams like a surgeon might insert a shunt into his patient, unanesthetized?

Should we note that the concrete foundation of a house is like the roots of a tree, like the arteries of a heart, like the bronchi of the lungs? Should we note that the long, jostling trip on the dollies to the used-house lot is like walking over stones with broken shins?

And if we do note these things, will the house appreciate the acknowledgment or will it stare unblinking at the other used houses in the dusty gravel lot?

And if the house stares unblinking at the other used houses in the dusty gravel lot, is it thinking of the houses it has left behind, its brother and sister houses on that handsome, settled old street with its whispery trees? Is the house reflective in this way, heavy with grief up and down the pinewood of its spine, or is it thinking about where it will go next, who will inhabit it, wondering—philosophically—about its purpose?

Does it stay awake at night, watching the sky and listening to the other houses murmur? Does it sleep?

And if it doesn't sleep, is this when the haunting begins, with insomnia, exhaustion gathering like shadows or hunger in the house's nonexistent basement?

And if the haunting *begins*, must it end?

And if the haunting must end, must it culminate noisily, in violence?

And if it must, should we skip ahead to an embodiment of innocence, a small, curious, faultless something that tempts and emphasizes the severity of this violence? Should we establish some gothic similarity, a balance, like that between twins? A similarity between this our chosen house and this our chosen frailty—for, after all, what is the uprooting of architecture if not the cutting away of memory, soft like childhood, at its knees?

Should we take this little girl staring out the car window as our example of innocence? And if we do take this little girl, with the ponytail and high socks, chin cupped in her hand, as our example, should we note that she has also been uprooted from her home, placed in a car and sent speeding down the highway outside Toronto with her parents, heading bullet-fast toward the TransCanada, toward a new city, a fresh start?

Should we note that her grandparents cried after they hugged her goodbye that morning, heartbroken to see her little body retreating down the driveway and into the vehicle? Will it matter to expose these details?

And if it will matter, *if it makes a difference*, should we expose the detail that the little girl's parents with their dark, tired eyes are also heartbroken to be leaving but feel they have no choice, that this move is necessary for the family's psychological survival? Should we describe the hurried glances they toss at the rearview mirror and their daughter in the backseat?

(Should we hint at the incident, or perhaps the series of incidents, that occurred at the little girl's school, the court case that has recently been resolved? And if we do hint at the incident, will the little girl be happy that we have provided context for her character and future actions, or will she disturb the protocol of parenthetical observations and turn to scowl at us off the page?)

And if she turns to scowl at us, should we return in embarrassment or alarm to our chosen house, sufficiently haunted but still unable to stare us down so easily, growing old and full of aches in the used-house lot?

Does the house look different? We've only been gone a minute, yet doesn't it look stretched and tall with anticipation or worry? Doesn't it look harried with its shutters pulled up tight into their window frames and the front door gripped by the surrounding walls? Would you believe that while we have been away a young couple has come to the used-house lot and spoken seriously with Dave of Dave's Movers himself, a young couple that has just bought a plot of land on which they would like to place a home? Would you believe they have wandered the lot and eventually chosen our chosen house, falling for its whimsical framing, something in its shape reminding the young woman of her grandfather's house where she used to vacation as a child?

And would you then believe that the house has overheard the young couple speaking with Dave, that it's preoccupied with its upcoming transition, that instead of joining the young couple it would very much like to go back to its old plot of land with its old humans inside of it (and really they were *old* humans, one dying silently in his bed and the other having a heart attack after she climbed a ladder to the attic to clean)? Will the house, in its preoccupation, resignedly comply with the transition, or will it resist with a loosening of all the nails in its woodwork while being loaded onto the truck?

And if it resignedly complies while being loaded onto the truck, dollies straining, will this attitude provoke the haunting to grow faster inside of the house, widening like a stain? Will the haunting sink deeper into the empty space behind cupboards and the cracks under doors as the knowledge sinks into the house that it is mobile but unable to move?

And, in the moment that the truck shudders onto the highway and the house creaks beneath an underpass, watching Southwestern Ontario farm fields roll into view for the first time, will the little girl, on this same highway, think the same thing? Will she look down at her motionless feet and consider them in contrast with the static blur of roadside out the window?

Will she look at the backs of her parents' heads, mother sleeping, father with hands on the steering wheel? Will she look back down at her shoes? Is she thinking of school? The tall people asking her questions? The nice woman with the pencil skirt and clipboard? That same woman in the hallway with her mother afterward, thinking the girl couldn't hear: *What has she said to you, exactly? Can't she explain in plain words—simple words, straightforward, how children generally, and in my experience, communicate—what has happened to her? Can you talk to her again, make her understand why it's essential, legally speaking, that she make a statement?*

Now in the car, while examining her own shoes and her own guilt, measuring that emotion for volume and viscosity, density and weight, will the girl take into consideration the fact, as an adult would, that she is barely nine years old?

Who will she blame?

Does she know *how* to blame and not hold everything like a stranger's exhalation in a tied balloon inside of her? Taut and unyielding as the haunting inside a house?

And as the little girl begins to learn how to blame as a self-protective measure, will her thoughts distract her from the huge, lumbering truck taking up the right-hand—and some of the center—lane of the highway, or will she look out the window as her father signals and moves to the left?

And if she looks out the window, will her eyes scan the length of the truck, which is also the length of the house strapped on top of it, or will they settle instead on the sign stuck to its back—CAUTION, WIDE LOAD—that warns drivers to slow for this behemoth traveling at fifty kilometers per hour down the highway?

And if her eyes scan the length of the truck, which is also the length of the house, will the house look back at her?

And if the house looks back at the little girl, will it study and memorize her small face in the car window—eyes globular and mouth pouched—out of boredom or in recognition of impending significance?

And if the house studies and memorizes her face out of boredom, will it be disappointed to admit that it is bored? Why doesn't its mortar crack finitely with excitement, or perhaps terror? Why doesn't the house anticipate? Why don't the screws connecting its pine frame register the torsion of their alarm, stress either physical or emotional, *something*, from being in transit?

And if it must admit that during the most interesting episode of its existence as a house, traveling along the highway to an unknown destination, it is bored and apathetic, must it also admit, must it conclude from this experience, that there is scant difference between movement and stagnation, mobility and domesticity, going *there* or staying *here*? Must it admit that everything follows: banality and frustration, humor, discontent, intrigue, disgust? That here on the truck on the highway it is still an old house, sour with memory, reluctant to open its doors?

And will these thoughts persist?

Will they scrape like a long fingernail on the underside of the house's attic roof, where it believes its brain to be, making it itch?

Will the house shift on top of the truck bed, restless, watching scattered hay bales turn into thicker and thicker forest, cottage country crowding in from the north?

Will the thoughts persist as an hour goes by, sun dropping almost to the horizon? Will they persist as the truck turns into a rest-stop parking lot, fills up on gas, and then occupies an entire line of parking spaces while the driver climbs down from his seat, stretches, and trundles inside to the washroom and to the Tim Hortons, where he will stand in line for twenty minutes to get his coffee?

And will the house, as it waits for the driver, look around the parking lot and notice the little girl sitting with her parents at a picnic table, squishing a sandwich made of white bread, cheese, and bologna into her mouth?

And if the house notices the little girl sitting with her parents, will it hold its breath as if underwater as it watches her, deriving vague comfort from the thoughtlessness and ease of her expression and movements, or will it exhale through its window frames and release a dark belly wind across the parking lot?

And if the house releases a dark belly wind, will the little girl smell the house's belly breath beyond the smell of her sandwich and look up to see and recognize the house, or will she not smell anything, transfixed by a ladybug that has just landed on the crust of her bread?

And if she looks up to see and recognize the house, will she think she has never seen anything quite as beautiful in her short life—the sun setting on the house's cyclopean window and vehicles flung by on the highway behind it?

And if she thinks that she has never seen anything quite as beautiful, will she turn back to her sandwich and the ladybug maneuvering onto her thumb, deciding there has been enough trouble lately and she doesn't need to make more, or will she follow this feeling of wonderment and detect a secret hushing want blooming up in her chest, deciding there has been enough trouble lately to justify one single, selfish act of curiosity?

(And will she think once more of the trouble, deep and snug inside her body like an intestinal bubble moving through her bowels? Will she see it all again, abruptly, like a fetid hiccup in her brain? The classroom and the questions and her wordlessness? The woman with her pen hesitating above the clipboard like a guillotine? *And then what did he make you do? And then—?* But how could she explain? How could she understand that something had been done to her when she was the one—in a technical sense—who had done the doing?

And then—?

And after that—?

And will the girl wonder why the people, all of them—the nice woman and the men, the police officers, the principal, the Ontario Teachers' Federation representative, her mother and father—couldn't and still can't hear her when she talks with her eyes and her silent hot throat and her lungs sticking up under her collarbones? Weren't they listening? Aren't they listening? Is it quiet for them in their heads and full, a wind tunnel, like it is for her, like it must be?

How could they ask her to speak—to say anything definitively?)

And if, looking at the house, she follows this feeling of wonderment and want, deciding there has been enough trouble lately to justify, after all, any act she might commit, will she put down her sandwich and tell her parents she's going to look at the house, or will she tell them her legs are sore and she's going to walk in the grass near where they've parked their car?

And if she tells her parents her legs are sore and she's going to walk in the grass, does this little lie, this fib, make her swell with self-sufficiency, does she feel strangely free, powerful, and autonomous as she stands and moves away from the picnic table?

And will this sensation of autonomy give her bravado enough to shift out of her parents' sight and dodge between stationary vehicles in the parking lot?

And if she shifts out of sight from her parents and dodges between stationary vehicles, will she be fearful as she approaches the house from the other side, or will she feel exhilarated, reverent, her heart jumping to hit the back of her throat like a mallet?

And if she's exhilarated, reverent, will the house feel this emotion and soak it up, boredom displaced—will the house and the girl regard each other seriously from their positions in the parking lot?

Will something like awe, a feeling close to comprehension, shift between them, a transference, like an athlete shifting weight from foot to foot?

And will the little girl move suddenly with assurance, without doubt or hesitation, without even looking around to see who could be watching, clambering up the side of the truck and reaching for the house's front doorknob, thinking, *This is control of chaos*, but not knowing what the thought means; or will she think of her parents at the picnic table and wonder whether or not they have finished their sandwiches, if they have headed back to the car, if they have grown suspicious? What will they do when they find her gone?

And if the little girl clambers up the side of the truck and reaches for the house's front doorknob, thinking, *This is con-*

trol of chaos, will the house, in shock and fear, seal itself against her intrusion, or will it unlock its door to receive her?

And if the house unlocks its door to receive her, will the girl swing herself inside and snap the door shut behind her, or will she pause and look into its shadow-darkened front entryway and feel that her curiosity has ebbed—will she go no further?

And if the girl swings herself inside and snaps the door shut behind her, does she hear a finality in this snapping shut or is her adrenaline thrumming so fervent and demanding through her system that she can't register anything wrong with the house and its pictureless walls, empty rooms, and echoing linoleum? And if her adrenaline—her heart in her mouth, beneath her tongue—distracts her, will she notice anything worth noticing or will her eyes skim jittering through the dim light? Will she see the floors tilted crazily to the side, aligned with the bed of the truck, or the cupboard doors in the kitchen tied shut like bound mouths so they don't flap open during the drive, or the framed entrance to what used to be the basement staircase now leading nowhere? Will she feel the humid thickness of vacancy circling her torso and limbs? Will she smell the mothy smoke of disturbed dust? Will she hear the low hush of highway traffic and nothing else, her ears submerged in the quiet that gathers between dense walls? Will she peek into each room as she passes it, the bathroom startling her backward when she sees her own eyes reflected darkly in the mirror on the wall?

Will the girl, as she reaches the staircase to the second floor, begin to know that the house is haunted in the same way a person begins to know while standing outside that it will rain? And if she doesn't know that the house is haunted, shall we call her continuing up to the second floor an act of naïveté, carelessness, stupidity? And if she does know that the house is haunted, if she has begun at least to sense, to suspect, shall we call her continuing up to the second floor an act of recklessness, defiance, fascination?

And if the house senses that the girl senses the haunting, will it want to explain itself to her as she ascends the stairs, will it try to speak with a shuffling of wind outside the window, or will it recognize its limits in terms of language and decide to show her, instead, drawing her into the master bedroom with the well-timed creaking of a floorboard?

And if the girl hears the creaking floorboard, will she think there's someone else in the house or will she think she has caused the creaking herself, some strange domino effect in the woodwork of the building?

And if she thinks there is someone else in the house, why does she drift almost dreamlike into the master bedroom as if she's floating or sleepwalking? Is she really that curious or has something else come over her, something like lucid memory, a quiet room perfect for privacy, a finger held over her mouth, pushed into her mouth, the fluorescent lights of a classroom?

And if something like lucid memory has come over her, are you surprised that her movements now are less decided and more instinctual?

And if you are not surprised that her movements now are more instinctual, will you yell at her to stop because you know what comes next?

And if you yell at her to stop because you know what comes next, will she hear you or will your voice blend with the distant sound of highway traffic outside the window?

And if your voice blends with the distant sound of highway traffic, will the girl enter the master bedroom unheeded?

And if the girl enters the master bedroom unheeded, will she see clearly—for once! Clarity!—because there is nothing else in the room, the attic hatch set into the ceiling, just above the bedroom window?

And if she sees the attic hatch set into the ceiling, will she cross the room and climb onto the windowsill, wedging her feet into the window frame and pressing her toes into the glass?

And if she crosses the room and climbs onto the windowsill, will she strain upward for the attic hatch (hearing something, thrumming, deep inside)?

And if she strains upward for the attic hatch, will she just be able to reach, or, too short, will she uselessly claw the invisible air?

And if she's just able to reach, will she push the hatch aside and hook her fingers around the wooden frame of the opening?

And if she pushes the hatch aside and hooks her fingers around the wooden frame of the opening, will she gather all her strength and kick off the windowsill, launching herself upward and into the attic? Will she scramble for a moment uncertainly, all limbs and uncoordinated, until her knees collide with the wooden frame and she's able to yank herself fully into the attic?

Will she crouch, still and attentive, staring into the dark attic, a sour smell rising up, listening to something that we can't hear?

Will silence ensue?

Will silence ensue, the master bedroom empty and gray and numb?

Will silence ensue, the highway far away full of cars and the sun sinking lower?

Will the girl's whisper break the silence, floating downward: *What? No—can't you hear me? Can't you come closer?*

Will silence ensue?

Will her whisper break again—*No. No, I don't want to.*

Will a shifting sound fall from the open attic hatch, a scuffling, some kind of altercation, a sharp whimper? What does she see? In the dark, empty attic, what does she see?

Does the house act, or does it simply unroll, let loose, as the girl begins to shriek?

Does it derive pleasure from this moment as the girl loses her footing and falls backward, quickly as if pushed? Does it wince or look on steadfastly as her body curves and she strikes the floor, sending a crunch and then a snapping sound out into the air, echoing briefly through the furnitureless room, ricocheting off the closed window? And if the house looks on steadfastly, does it now try to look away as the girl's body unfolds and she lies limp, neck twisted, eyes open and chin tilted up to the ceiling?

And if the house tries to look away as the girl's body unfolds, does it find that it cannot—no matter how purposefully it focuses its gaze on the horizon and the blazing sunset—because her body is inside of it, like a piece of debris stuck in its eyeball, its mind's eye?

Will the house count to ten to rid itself of the girl's stillness and the unnatural turn of her spine?

And if the house counts to ten, will this countdown be the last ten seconds that the truck driver spends in the Tim Hortons line, and will he shamble out now with cup in hand, hoisting himself up into the driver's seat?

And if he shambles out now with cup in hand, hoisting himself up into the driver's seat, will the girl's parents pause as they pack up the cooler on top of the picnic table to watch the house drive away and ease onto the highway? Will they watch it until it's gone, moving with that same steady, frustrating, unstoppable patience that most common and horrible things in life acquire, growing smaller, less sufficient, trudging on?

ARTHUR, HUSHA, AND NELLIE pause in tableau in the midsummer heat, which is hot enough that they had to open all the windows—although Husha protested, she would rather the heat than the noise from the cicadas—and close all the blinds. The house sinks into half shadow. Arthur is alone in his room, sitting in a chair by the window, sighing loudly. The breezes through the window are occasional and brief, but the buzz-sawing of cicadas is relentless, unyielding. Husha protests again, says it's worse, the sound is much worse than the warmth. Her hands come up to her ears. Sweat from her neck cuffs the sides of her wrists. She's standing in the archway between the kitchen and the hall that leads down to the bedrooms, bathroom, and laundry room. The hardwood floor is smooth, almost buttery, beneath her bare feet. The sound of the cicadas grinds down into her eardrums. She wears a pair of shorts and a sports bra and is glistening. She turns slowly in a circle, like a planet rotating, and whines from the back of her throat.

Nellie, lying on her back on the couch, her arms flung over her head and draped against the armrest, looks languidly at Husha from between the arches of her similarly bare feet, which are propped on the other end of the couch.

Go to the bedroom, then, offers Nellie, and bake yourself to death in there. Alone. You're not closing the windows in here. In actuality, she wants Husha to stay. She watches Husha leaning against the wall, where Husha perhaps hopes to peel some coolness, some relief, onto her skin from the plaster. She's rosy, dewy, shoulders round and scooping up into her neck, stomach pouched a little around the belly button and thinning out toward the hips, skin on the inward slope of her thighs supple, creamy like pudding—Nellie catches the thought as it leaves her head and almost laughs at herself, almost laughs aloud at having landed on such a description, imagining Husha as a food she might consume, or at least consisting of parts that resemble foods she might consume. Dismembering or disembodying Husha in this way startles her, makes her want to laugh in order to brush the thought away, pretend at nonchalance. She never sees Husha this bare, this exposed, in daylight. Her body is heated and feminine. Husha is so unaware.

* * * *

OKAY, says Nellie, okay. I have one to add, now that I really know what kind of story we're going for. I think your mom would like this one.

Sure, says Husha. She's cross-legged on the carpet, in long socks, sitting next to her grandfather's chair. She hooks her hands around the tops of her feet and pulls backward, stretching out her shins. Her glasses, the ones she only takes out for reading, driving, or watching movies, are pushed up into her hair. With her eyes, Nellie measures the angle of Husha's collarbone disappearing into her T-shirt.

What? asks Husha, watching Nellie watch her.

Nothing, says Nellie. She pulls her feet beneath her on the couch.

Arthur grunts. His face is turned sideways, long nose in profile, staring out at the black window. He never looks like he's listening, rarely shows any sign of attention, of interest, and then later he will produce details from the stories that neither Nellie nor Husha remember telling or hearing. Like a kid playing with toys in the other room, thinks Nellie, and swallowing every bit of his parents' conversation.

Husha is half-smiling across the coffee table. Well? she asks.

Well, says Nellie, the story is about my stepdad, Henry. But really it's about stepdads everywhere. She straightens her shoulders and raises one index finger in mock ceremony. I would like to formally propose it as an addition to the collection, she says, because I believe stepdads get a bad rap, especially in literature. It's high time we had a new, more radical depiction of the stepdad: stepdad as charming, as trickster, as martyr, sacrificing even his fingers for the family.

Husha chokes on the tea that she has just brought to her mouth. Arthur arches an eyebrow.

This story begins, says Nellie, relaxing back into the couch, on the morning of my eighth birthday party, April first.

Husha frowns. Is this a fictional story? she asks. I know your birthday isn't April first.

Arthur unfolds his hands, splaying them palms-up across his lap. Birthday *party*, he declares.

Right, says Nellie. Arthur's got it. The devil's in the details. I was born on March twenty-eighth, as you know, but weekdays happen to be inconvenient for an eight-year-old's birthday party, so we celebrated on the Saturday—April first.

Okay, says Husha. Okay, I get it.

The date is important, says Nellie, and requires emphasis. All that morning, while my mom ran around preparing for the party, which would start at the roller-skating rink and finish at the house, my stepdad, Henry, had been playing April Fool's

Day pranks, and it was driving my mom nuts. He started by sneaking into my room before I woke and covering my bedroom doorknob with toothpaste, so I couldn't leave without getting toothpaste all over my hands. Then he taped a fake cockroach onto the inside of the toilet bowl. Then he changed the salt out for sugar, pretended he had broken my mom's favorite clay salad bowl, and, most impressively, convinced me that a hot-air balloon had landed in our neighbor's yard and I should bring the camera—quick!—only to find the neighbor's teenage son sunbathing shirtless. By the time Henry had turned the cake icing the color green (claiming, when my mom confronted him, that he did it for my love of *Shrek*), and tied two of my friends' roller-skate laces together, my mom's face was shifting between deep red and what I would describe as a patchy oatmeal-gray. We drove home from roller skating with Avril Lavigne shouting out of the radio, and Henry dancing in the front seat as he steered the car in a wobbly line, mid-lane, making us all giggle and shriek. My mom was quiet in the passenger seat, and when we were welcomed into the house by our two yappy dogs, Samson the Pomeranian and Mac the bulldog-terrier mix, Mom sent both dogs and stepdad out into the backyard, muttering something about "that damn Playhouse."

And this—ah—the Playhouse. Well. I probably should have mentioned it earlier. Henry loved to build things, and to fix things, which I guess falls into the stepdad cliché. The problem was, ever since he and my mom combined their incomes and rented a nicer place in the north end of the city, there wasn't all that much left to fix, and there wasn't anything that needed building. So Henry took his tools and a stack of wood into the backyard and began work on his Playhouse, which was like a shed but less sturdy, with lots of tiny rooms and makeshift benches and a ladder that led to the roof, where he would sit and dangle his legs and smoke cigarettes during the nice weather. He was always in the middle of adding something to the Playhouse, whether it was nailing a new shelf to the wall or carving out a new door or sanding down a three-legged desk. (Four legs are boring, he once told me. Everything around here has four legs.) The Playhouse was sprawling and, along with Henry's workbench and tools, now took up at least half of the backyard. My mom was surprisingly fond of it, despite her attempts to convince everyone otherwise. She would often proclaim it an eyesore, and then go out with her paints and brushes and add to the mural she had started on the back wall.

Some days, however, like this one, she was simply happy that the Playhouse kept my stepdad busy. He put on his boots and went out with the dogs and in two minutes we could hear, faintly through the glass back door, the sound of his drill drilling and his hammer hammering and his saw sawing. My mom sighed, and we all sat down to the predictability of opening presents and eating the green cake.

Ten minutes later, as my mom was sucking icing off the ends of each of the eight candles, Henry appeared at the back door. He had taken off his shirt and wrapped it around his hand. He bumped his shoulder against the glass. My friends turned and stared.

Hey, he said. We could hear him muffled through the glass. Hey. I cut off my finger.

My mom sat for a moment with her mouth open, and then she stood and walked to the door. We all watched, hands still around our forks, as she reached down and turned the lock.

Not funny, she said through the glass.

Annie! Henry shouted. Annie!

Give it up, she said. I've had enough.

My mom turned away and started cleaning the kitchen, gathering plates and putting the rest of the cake in Tupperware. She only stopped when one of my friends screamed, pointing toward the backyard. Henry had unwrapped his hand. His palm was covered in blood and the tip of his middle finger was missing.

Okay! my mom said. Okay! She flung open the back door and let Henry inside, handing him a paper towel and a bag of frozen peas. She got midway through calling an ambulance before saying, Oh, fuck it, and dragged Henry out to the car. My friends and I were silent, watching from the front window as the car backed out of the driveway. Eventually I went into the kitchen and started wiping the drops of blood off the floor with the shirt my stepdad had left on the table.

When the phone rang, I felt cold and tired, like I'd woken from a long nap. I could hear my friends whispering in the other room.

Hello?

Oh, honey, hi, said my mom.

Is Henry okay?

Oh, honey, he's fine. Just fine. How are your friends?

We're all right.

That's good, that's good. Thanks for being such a big girl about all of this. I just have one more big-girl thing for you to do.

I breathed in for a long time. Then out. Okay, I said.

First, I need you to get a bucket from the garage and fill it with all the ice from the freezer, okay?

Okay, I said.

Can you do that for me now?

Mm-hm. I left the phone on the counter and I went to the garage and got a bucket and pulled a chair over from the table and stood on it and filled the bucket with all the ice from the freezer.

Now, said my mom, I need you to go into the backyard and—and—well, I need you to find Henry's finger. Once you find it, I need you to put it in the ice. Can you do that for me?

My friends had wandered back into the kitchen and were looking at me, wondering about the ice, waiting to see what would happen next.

Last big-girl thing, my mom said. Promise.

Okay, I said.

I left the phone on the counter again and went out to the backyard and down the porch steps to Henry's workbench. I looked on top and I looked underneath, I looked inside the Playhouse and in the grass, but I couldn't find his finger anywhere. It was only on my way back inside that I noticed something funny. Samson and Mac were in the back corner of the yard, very quiet and preoccupied.

Samson! I said. Mac!

Samson turned to look at me, but Mac had his nose in the dirt. By the time I got to him, his big, wide tongue was licking his lips.

* * * *

HUSHA IS laughing with her hands over her face. And that's what we're going for? she asks, breathless. Arthur has leaned back in his chair and closed his eyes.

What? says Nellie.

You said, "Now that I know what we're going for." You said, "I think your mom would like this one."

I think she would! says Nellie. She holds up her hands in defense.

There's such a thing as a theme, you know. Continuity? Tone?

Nellie rolls her eyes. Come on, she says. You didn't even let me get to the best part.

And what's that?

Well, says Nellie, you would think having one less finger would be beneficial in certain ways. Convenient, for example, when trimming your nails.

Sure, says Husha. Her eyes narrow in a playful squint.

Not for poor Henry. He chopped off his finger right before the nail bed, so the nail still grows out to the length of a normal finger if he's not diligent.

Gross! Husha shouts, and leans back against her grandfather's chair.

Arthur, in his apparent slumber, smirks.

Swamp Woman

IN A CITY IN ONTARIO—not the big city, Toronto, or the other notable city, Ottawa, but a city nonetheless, surrounded by small towns like spots of acne around the core of infection—Wife Emily was sitting down in the kitchen to dinner, which was a pot of sticky macaroni and cheese. Wife Emily was small with an unassuming look to her long forehead and tucked chin. Her hands were petite, each fingernail painted a week ago with the paint now chipping off. The way she laced her fingers together and pulled them toward her stomach while waiting for her dinner to cool betrayed apprehension, uncertainty, a reluctance to engage with the materiality of the house around her, to admit to the reality of her body in the world. Even here in the private space of her own home—perhaps *especially* here in the private space of her own home—this apprehension pervaded Wife Emily like cold water leaking up through her nostrils and then down her throat. A cyclical sensation, a dripping, a gathering of liquid unwillingness inside of her, calm in its rhythmic building, and yet like suspense, containing a violent thrashing deep and invisible somewhere near her stomach, lodged against her spine, beneath her lungs.

Wife Emily was tired. She knew the macaroni and cheese in front of her on the table would only make her more tired, but she didn't have the energy or the ingredients in the fridge to make a more digestible meal. She was a mother as well as a wife, and she had already put her best efforts into caring for Little Jenny that morning. That morning? Wasn't it now late afternoon? Wife Emily was a timekeeper as well as a wife and mother, but she hadn't done well with keeping the time lately; it seemed determined to remain unkempt, slipping away from her in the way wind slipped through the fingers of tree branches, the way fish slipped through water—the way thoughts slipped in and around heads and out ears.

Wife Emily sensed her metaphors growing convoluted, saw, in her mind's eye, fish entwined, curling into the crescent shape of ears, the fingers of tree branches blooming up underwater.

She shook herself, tossing her head sharply on top of her spinal column.

Wife Emily was—used to be—a sister and an aunt as well as a wife. Her sister, Kathy, had died recently at the bottom of a lake in a campsite just outside the city. She had drowned with her daughter, Niece Theodora, who was only seven years old—a strange occurrence considering the weather was fine and the water was calm and they could both swim. But sometimes strange things happen, Wife Emily reasoned, to regular people, even the unassuming ones, the nonconfrontational, those who go about minding their own business. The deaths of her sister and niece had been one of many recent upsets in Wife Emily's life, along with Husband Jack leaving on his important, very much imperative work trip and Little Jenny's expected but intrusive arrival, which all occurred around the same time: first the deaths, then the birth, and then the husband three months later or so, or so, striding out the front door, a bit of a half wave, a bit of a half death, as he went. The deaths (she remembered the funeral, the strained chords of organ music as she walked down the aisle, thoughts swimming, Little Jenny's body bearing down inside her own, the wide steps down the aisle, swimming, the sun above the lake, bodies dragged from the water), the work trip, the baby—it was all enough to make Wife Emily forget herself now and then, to forget that her hands were connected by wrists to her arms and her arms by shoulders to her body, to forget what her skin felt like over her bones while she moved, and to forget, occasionally, Little Jenny too.

She looked down at her macaroni and cheese, and then Wife Emily—

—stepped out of the shower and thought for a moment that she would call Sister Kathy to help with Little Jenny that day (where was Little Jenny, anyway?), but she remembered a moment later that Sister Kathy was dead with Niece Theodora and no one would be home to answer the telephone but grieving Brother-in-Law George. Her feet sank into the thick bathmat outside the shower, herself sinking into what she supposed was loneliness but what felt simply like vacancy inside of her. She drew a towel from the rack to dry herself and noted how soggy and huge the hot shower had made her feel. In reality she was petite. Husband Jack often called her petite. In reality she looked small standing in most rooms and had difficulty announcing her presence. From her vantage point, however, the shower had made her massive, her thighs stretching to the floor beneath her—flabby, all rubber skin, rouged. Her eyes melted into her cheekbones in her reflection in the dripping bathroom mirror.

Staring at herself, she was unsurprised, underwhelmed: everything these days made her feel heavy and slow.

Little Jenny began to cry in the next room (ah, of course, in her crib), her voice low and gurgling down the hallway like the start of a siren passing through water. If Husband

Jack had been home from his business trip, Wife Emily would have called for him to help her, to soothe the baby if he were able, if he wasn't already busy. But Husband Jack wouldn't be home for two more days, and two days was still a long time, time long enough to bend, widen, and warp. Wife Emily supposed she would get through it. Little Jenny wailed and wailed as Wife Emily stepped out of the bathroom, and then Little Jenny began to cough, choking for a moment before Wife Emily opened the bedroom door and reached into the crib. She hadn't bothered to put clothes on or wrap herself in the towel, so she stood naked by the window with the baby in her arms, rocking her back and forth. Little Jenny soon hiccupped and quieted and found Wife Emily's breast. Together they sat on the floor against the wall, one in the arms of the other, and fell asleep.

Before Wife Emily slipped entirely into unconsciousness and away from the room filled with drifts of steam still leaking from the bathroom down the hall, she imagined that the heady scent of her milk was filling her eyes, as stagnant as swamp water, lake water, the muddy undercurrent of insensibility.

She woke to Little Jenny crying again, trying to wriggle out of her arms and onto the floor.

Hush, she crooned, pulling Little Jenny back up against her shoulder. Wife Emily was expert at crooning and calming. She thought of Husband Jack's stricken face, the way he sometimes woke in the middle of the night from what he claimed were indescribable dreams. Shaking, covering his eyes, not letting Wife Emily touch him as if she were a stranger, he would turn to the side and wonder if this had all been a mistake. All what? she would ask. If all what had been a mistake? You don't understand the kind of stress I'm under, he would reply quietly, like a prayer.

As a wife, it was crucial that she be expert at crooning and calming. Soothing another human being was a banal activity, to be sure, but it was also simple, rudimentary, her mind floating elsewhere while she produced the proper sounds—*shhh, okay, I know, I know*—and performed the necessary actions—rubbing his shoulders, getting him a glass of water or an extra blanket—to send her husband back into slumber. Being a mother, she discovered with disappointment, wasn't much different. A confounding combination: while using all her energy, her whole self, motherhood required little more than the ability to settle states of disequilibrium: when the baby was noisy, she quieted her; when the baby was hungry, she fed her; when the baby was dirty, she cleaned her; when the baby was tired, she made her sleep.

Wife Emily hooked her forearm under Little Jenny's bottom. The air was warm, and her skin was oily with sweat. Her neck ached from her head hanging down as she slept. She tried to stretch it out, rotating it from side to side, and registered, as she turned her head, a sound coming from the doorway, from the bathroom down the hall, the pulse of running water. She rose staggeringly to her feet.

The shower was running hot when she entered the bathroom. The curtain had been pulled aside and water speckled the bathmat and floor. Wife Emily skidded on the slick linoleum and nearly lost her grip on Little Jenny, but caught herself on the corner of the sink. She shut off the water and stood staring through the foggy air, finding her balance.

Hadn't she turned the shower off before getting out?

She held the baby to her chest with one hand and with the other held her head. She looked up at the mirror, and then Wife Emily—

—was standing in the kitchen, either the day before or the day after she had found the shower running. She was standing with the fridge door open, listening to footsteps upstairs and trying to remember whom she had invited over, maybe her friends and their children, who were older than Little Jenny and could already walk, maybe her sister and niece. No, she corrected herself—no. But the footsteps were quick and slapping, insistent, like raindrops striking a glass window. The rest of the house was quiet. Wife Emily looked at her hand holding open the fridge door and wondered where she had left Little Jenny.

Jenny? she called toward the ceiling. She still found it odd, somehow dishonest, to call her baby by a name that could belong to an adult. She recognized that she was, in fact, the odd one, made uneasy by this ordinary and altogether unremarkable ritual of name-calling. She was the odd one, wasn't she? Imagining that Little Jenny shouldn't have a name, that she wasn't a real person or at least couldn't someday become one. Wife Emily laughed at the idea of ever calling her child Jennifer. Where had this name come from, anyway? What was its genesis? Wife Emily vaguely recalled Husband Jack mentioning some beloved childhood friend with this name. *Jennifer*—how unexceptional, much like her own name, which she had always felt uncomfortable using to identify herself. In her opinion, her parents had done a bad job with naming their children; Sister Kathy had hated her name and frequently tried out variations of the lengthy and austere *Katherine*: Kate, Kat, Kath. She once attempted to convince the family to call her Rinn. And perhaps this concern for labels was why she came up with the name Theo for her own child, a name not unheard-of but which caught the ear, settled and focused the brain for a moment. *Theodora*: now, that was a name worth rolling around one's mouth.

The footsteps, which had been pounding down what sounded to Wife Emily like the upstairs hallway, stopped directly above her head in Little Jenny's bedroom. But Little Jenny was too young to walk, let alone pound down a hallway. Wife Emily felt suddenly nauseous, knew for certain she hadn't invited anyone over, no friends and no children. She ran in a fog up the stairs. When she reached the top, the hallway floor pressed warmly into her bare feet and the air was slimy with steam. Had she left the shower running? Apparently so—hot mist crowded out of the bathroom door and coated the walls in large, rubbery droplets.

Through the bedroom door in front of her, Wife Emily could see that Little Jenny was not in her crib or playpen. Damp smudges like footprints dotted the carpeted floor. She felt her hair clammy against the back of her neck. Wife Emily went down the hall and into the bathroom and found Little Jenny lying on her back in the fast-filling tub, the shower pelting her small body. The drain had been plugged, the water had reached Little Jenny's ears, but the baby seemed unperturbed: she lay quietly looking upward at the ceiling, her mouth pinched in an *o* almost the same size and shade of pink as Wife Emily's thumbnail. Little Jenny's belly was round, poking just above the water and wiggling as she kicked her legs. If Wife Emily loved anything about her daughter it was this, her round, smooth belly like a chunk of stretched dough—firm, cohesive, pristine.

Wife Emily remembered suddenly that she should scream. Jenny! That she should act, react, that she still played a part in the scene unfolding before her. Her voice when she yelled sounded far away, as if spoken from another mouth across the room. As she yanked her daughter from the bathtub and turned off the hot water, Little Jenny gurgled and laughed and spit in her face. Wife Emily watched as the last of the bathwater swung down the drain, leaving a brown ring of sludge or mold around the base of the tub. Dirty, filthy—when had her home become so unclean? She made a mental note to scrub the bath later. When? Later. The skin on Little Jenny's back was pink and raw, as if rubbed with sandpaper. Wife Emily rushed downstairs— needing to get out of that bathroom, her head feeling fuzzy and hot in that bathroom—where she placed the baby in the kitchen sink and ran cold water over her body.

Little Jenny shrieked.

Shhh, hush, said Wife Emily, clutching the baby's limbs. She stroked the little girl's back. She was expert at crooning and calming. She was expert at crooning and calming. She was expert at crooning and calming. She put her mouth on Little Jenny's ear and promised that Husband Jack would be home tomorrow, but she wasn't sure what day it was, wasn't sure if this promise was true. Shhh, she said. Hush now. Come on, now. Be quiet.

But Little Jenny wouldn't be quiet. She was resolute. She cried and cried and wouldn't stop unless she was left alone in her crib with Wife Emily a safe distance downstairs. Now this she had certainly never read about in her baby books, which had all been convenient hand-me-downs from Sister Kathy: a baby *not* wanting to be with its mother, requiring independence, desiring space. Wife Emily, sitting alone down in the kitchen, tapping her fingernails on the tabletop, felt her apathy dissolve, her chest tightening with an opaque anger that locked her tongue to the roof of her mouth. She looked up, looked at the light outside the kitchen window and couldn't decide if it was early morning or late evening. Everything dull and orange. Occasionally she heard what she thought were footsteps upstairs, bewilderingly inconsistent, sometimes rapid, childlike; sometimes heavy, thumping, slow. She began rapping herself on the top of her skull each time she heard the footsteps in order to knock the sound from her head. Little Jenny was quiet in her crib. Sleeping, in fact, when Wife Emily crept upstairs to check, her feet soft on each step.

Wasn't Little Jenny hungry?

Wasn't she cold?

Hadn't she soiled herself?

Wasn't she bored? Didn't she need entertainment? A change of scene? Intellectual engagement? Didn't she need to go outside? Physical activity? Stretch her limbs? Maintain some symmetry between her external and internal worlds? Achieve this equilibrium about which Wife Emily was so concerned? Was this balance unnecessary, after all? Could every action really be so inconsequential? Wife Emily watched Little Jenny sleep. Standing over the crib, she watched black spots like ants crawl across her vision. She felt compelled to reach down and push at Little Jenny's pale shoulder, make her cry, just to have something to do. She gripped the edge of the crib and resisted, and then Wife Emily—

—opened her eyes and the crying, the crying that she had heard loudly throughout a nightmare from which she was just now awakening, had subsided. She was lying on the floor with her hands over her ears, and Little Jenny had disappeared from the crib. Thick steam had filled the room, and as Wife Emily lifted herself from the floor and moved toward the doorway, she felt as if she were swimming through air. Swamp smog filled her lungs when she breathed, lake fronds tousled her hair. The unfamiliar shapes of furniture and picture frames bloomed out of the semi-darkness of the afternoon. Wife Emily floated past them, not recognizing them as objects until they were already behind her.

In the bathroom, the shower was running. A small, pink body struggled facedown in the bathtub, the sounds of her splashes drowned out by the water crashing into the tub from the showerhead. When Wife Emily lifted Little Jenny from the bath, the baby stared at her, unbreathing, her eyes shaking in her skull. Then she made a noise like a deep belch in her chest. She puked on Wife Emily's neck. Her round fingertips, opening and closing into fists, were wrinkled like tiny brains.

Wife Emily held Little Jenny at arm's length, her hands under her armpits and her fingers wrapping around the baby's back to support her head. She watched Little Jenny breathe, waited for her to cry, turned and studied her body, searching for evidence of harm. She didn't know whether or not she should call the doctor or take Little Jenny to the hospital, whether or not it was absolutely necessary Husband Jack know about the incident. For the first time in a long while, Wife Emily's thoughts felt sharp, her head clear as if emptied of cotton stuffing. It was not absolutely necessary, she decided, that Husband Jack should know. If it wasn't necessary for her to know precisely what he did on his business trips, then he didn't need to know about this. Wife Emily's body strengthened suddenly with elation, power, a sense of control. Her grip was firm on her baby's torso. She had the autonomy—if not the expertise—to diagnose. To her, Little

Jenny looked fine, breathed fine, her face tilted perhaps a little wanly against one shoulder. But still, absurdly, she didn't cry.

As Wife Emily watched her daughter, as steam clung densely to the tile walls, as the shower pounded on and on into the bathtub, and as the house hung quietly around them with the compression of oncoming evening, a sensation of tranquility descended upon Wife Emily—or if it wasn't tranquility, it was sedateness, complete and unassuming detachment, unconcern. She had the autonomy to diagnose, to decide; but, even more importantly, she had the autonomy to misdiagnose or to remain in indecision, to claim passivity as a worthwhile conclusion. She saw suddenly, clearly—like scraping mud from a pane of glass—order in the unkempt, dexterity in the uncoordinated, a sense of purpose in determined inaction. She was in control.

And in this moment of control a drop of brown liquid landed on top of Little Jenny's head and rolled into her eye socket.

The baby hiccupped. Wife Emily looked up.

A woman, or what used to be a woman, clung to the ceiling above the shower. Her hands and feet were spread wide like lizards' toes, and her head was at an odd angle, turned owl-like at the two of them below her. Her skin was a dull swamp green and hung from her in large, doughy sections, as if it weren't skin at all, but a loose, liquidy bag that the woman had stepped her skeleton into. Sparse coils of black hair hung from her skull, and a long string of drool swung from her bloated lips.

For a moment, Wife Emily thought she was looking in the mirror, upside down, but when she turned her head to the wall above the sink, she saw her own face staring back at her with wide, sunken eyes and frizzy hair. It was just that this woman, this creature on the ceiling, seemed familiar, something in the jawline and bridge of the nose mimicking her own. Then she realized the creature was Kathy, Sister Kathy, and as the woman detached herself from the ceiling and slopped onto the floor, Wife Emily ran from the room with Little Jenny in her arms. She slipped on the slick hardwood and went down, managing to swivel her body in midair so Little Jenny landed on top of her, head thumping softly between Wife Emily's breasts.

Wife Emily used her elbows to slide herself backward toward the stairs while the woman crawled out of the bathroom, her legs dragging limp behind her.

* * * *

LATER, Wife Emily called Brother-in-Law George and told him Sister Kathy was alive, but she was changed. Brother-in-Law George couldn't understand a word Wife Emily said—her voice was guttural and bubbling, her mouth emitting sounds that made his stomach turn. He assumed she had had a stroke. Brother-in-Law George called Husband Jack, who caught an early flight home from Toronto. He also called the police, who arrived to find Wife Emily sitting naked in an empty bathtub with Little Jenny fast asleep in her lap.

Wife Emily couldn't speak for two weeks. She thought she could—she told her story over and over to Husband Jack, to the nurses and doctors at the hospital, and finally to the psychiatrist, each time using only as much detail as she determined necessary, presenting a story appropriately believable. The sweaty cloud that had invaded her brain in the weeks previous had, since saving Little Jenny from drowning, dissolved. Sharp clarity had swallowed her up like a sky without precipitation, like a cold wind striking an open eyeball.

What the medical officials heard, what everyone heard, was a series of jumbled gurgles spurting from her mouth along with her saliva. Only Little Jenny seemed to understand any of it: during visits to the hospital, she was more attached to her mother than ever before, and she laughed when Wife Emily made her babbling noises—sometimes she even spoke back.

When Wife Emily did find her English words, she could do nothing more than explain that a woman had come out of the bathtub drain as a baby, smaller than a baby, a fetus, and had grown until she was Wife Emily's size, until she was dead, and had wanted to take Little Jenny with her, to play with Niece Theodora. When asked who this woman was, when prompted to explain that it was her trauma-informed conception of Sister Kathy, Wife Emily had no response. She had remembered how to communicate, but she had forgotten the "true words," as she called them. She decided not to tell anyone that her original description of the woman on the ceiling as Sister Kathy was overly simplistic, degrading in its precision. The truth, if there was such a thing, was more complex, burrowed within folds of disorientation, futility, like a tick with its head lodged in skin. Somewhere along the way, she assured her interrogators, she had lost the story. Husband Jack, Brother-in-Law George, and the psychiatrist were left to connect the strange and ill-formed pieces of narrative she provided, like building a body out of mismatched bone and flesh.

* * * *

MONTHS LATER, after recovering, Wife Emily would wake in the night and remember the whole thing, all of it, in a flash that kicked her breath from her throat and pulled her torso up out of bed.

The woman, the creature from the drain, had dragged herself through the hallway and taken Little Jenny from Wife Emily's arms. She had held her in the sludge between her swinging breasts and leaned back against the wall, her bruised legs sticking out into the middle of the hallway. She was not petite. She was enlarged, balloon-huge and heavy. She had rocked Little Jenny back and forth and fed her the green milk from her breasts and spoken to her in a language that Wife Emily couldn't understand.

Wife Emily lay in the hall on her belly and studied the woman's green body. She was sleepy, she was hungry, she was glad for the help with the baby. She played with the woman's toes, the moss growing between them, and asked her about endings and beginnings and the fear of these things. She was unconcerned now, couldn't find fear inside her when she thought of Sister Kathy at the bottom of the lake, Sister Kathy lying in the open casket, but she wasn't sure this was the same as being unafraid.

The swamp woman didn't hear her. Or—perhaps—she pretended not to listen.

In that moment, however, when Wife Emily would sit up in bed and remember the woman's face, her voice, her swampy milk, which Wife Emily had, when invited with a smile showing moldy teeth, drunk solemnly and with fervor beside Little Jenny, Husband Jack would lift himself onto an elbow beside her and say a word, softly, into the dark. The flash of comprehension and recollection would fade into the corners of the black bedroom, and Wife Emily would settle back onto her pillow, finding her voice in her throat, and whisper to Husband Jack that everything was fine, that they should go back to sleep.

ARTHUR AND HUSHA ARE in the bathroom together. The bathroom is long and narrow with a worn tile floor and gray countertops. The walls are olive green. There is rust at the base of the faucet in the sink. A speckling of mold on the underside of the countertop that Husha tries every so often to scrub off. Husha would never have noticed the mold, no one in the house would have known, if Arthur didn't sit so low down in the tub as he does now, able to look at the underside of countertops and what grows there. He sits in the tub with his back curved up against the ceramic and his waist, legs, and feet submerged beneath the soapy water. Husha, from where she leans against the wall near the towel rack, can only see a smudged outline of the lower half of his body. The skin of his chest hangs a little toward his stomach, loose around his skeleton. Sparse hairs, white and wiry, curl up from below his collarbones and the tops of his shoulders. His neck and forehead are flushed with heat. In his semi-reclined position, he stares up at the ceiling, where a long rectangle of sunlight, thrown up from the window, moves almost imperceptibly toward the door. The sun is setting. The bathroom door is closed. On the other side of the door is the hallway and down the hallway is the kitchen and then the living room, where Nellie lies on the couch with her head tilted back, replicating Arthur's posture in the bath, and scrolls methodically on her phone.

This is their routine every second or third day: after dinner, Husha runs a bath, waiting a minute before testing the water temperature with the back of her hand. If it's too hot, she adds a little cold—too cold, a little hot. She knows by now how her grandpa likes it. After another minute she leaves the room and Arthur enters. He closes the door and undresses. This part of the ritual, during which Arthur undresses alone, is a bit super-fluous because, in a moment, Arthur will pop the door open a crack and stand on the bathmat and Husha will reenter to help him into the tub. He's entirely naked, exposed—doesn't bother with a towel or to cover himself with his hands. In their bath routine, at least, Husha and Arthur have ventured beyond for-malities or embarrassment (the purpose of many formalities, after all, is to wear down the edge of embarrassment). Still, it's important to both of them that Arthur undress alone. In this small way, with the bathroom door closed, Arthur maintains his ability to care for himself, to complete personal and private tasks, like the taking off of clothes from his own body. In this small way his nudity remains his own choice, as he's the one who decides when he will pop the door open a crack and move across the room to the bathmat.

Husha, stepping gingerly back into the room after waiting outside, is fascinated by Arthur's body. He's grown accustomed to the way she looks at him. An outsider, invisibly entering the bathroom or peering into the window, might find her stare—the unapologetic hardness of it—disrespectful. Husha has told Arthur before that she loves the history she sees in his skin, the folds and doughy pouches, the places where hair grows pro-fusely or has ceased to grow at all. She remembers him from when she was younger, a little girl visiting the house on the lake during her summer holiday—the sturdiness of his body as he departed from middle age and arrived slowly at his elderly years. The width of his chest, the straight line of his spine, the way the elasticity disappeared bit by bit from the skin around his stomach but his muscles remained firm (he was a couple of years away from retiring and still did regular agricultural fieldwork on farms partnered with the university). The way he propelled himself up a flight of stairs. The way he trotted down the hill to the lake. The palms of his hands round like paddles as he picked her up, the weightlessness of her body in his arms. He wasn't objectively a large man, but he was tall, over six feet. Without her dad around Husha rarely interacted with men of any size, and as a result, all men felt huge to her: broad, overbearing, unaccommodating in their bodies' lack of curves, the hardness of their limbs and torsos. Her grandpa's saving grace, what drew her to him, were his sloping shoulders as he bent over a book; the way he dropped to his knees in the garden to test the dampness of the soil with his fingertips; his deep belly laughter in the kitchen in the morning; his silence and watchfulness while others were speaking; the tentative angle of his smile.

Now he stands naked on the bathmat in front of the granddaughter he used to swing around in his arms (here she is, standing in front of him in the bathroom doorway, having grown and changed just as much as he has, having lost her childhood lightness). He maintains his ability to care for himself by taking off his own clothes behind a closed door; he maintains his balance by resting one hand, however lightly, on the towel rack. He has lost so much of his old self—the stability and certainty of his body, occasionally his mind—but he holds on to the silence and watchfulness that Husha remembers so well, watching her watch him from the doorway.

You're looking skinny, says Husha. You should eat more.

Arthur shrugs, feeling the edge of a smile pull up the corner of his lip. He thinks twice about commenting on the quality of her cooking.

What? asks Husha, seeing his expression. What is it?

Nothing, says Arthur. He almost says, *None of your concern*, but then flinches away from this response, knows that Husha is still anxious about the forbidden box in his bedroom. Come on, he says, gesturing to the tub. Help me in.

So reticent, Husha mutters. She moves forward to guide him down into the water, clasping his elbow in her hand and pausing a moment so he can grip her bicep. Their forearms run along each other, their bones locked in place. When he leans back, she counter-leans, balancing his weight as he hoists his feet one by one over the lip of the tub, bends his knees, and lowers himself into the water.

They release each other in the same moment, indents from their fingertips remaining in the hollows of their elbows. Husha passes him the soap.

Thank you, he says. His spine finds the cool ceramic curve of the tub and he blows air out through his lips. The sun is setting and an orange rectangle of evening light begins its slow progression along the ceiling. Husha settles against the wall and crosses her arms. She doesn't leave, she never does, imagining him falling asleep and slipping beneath the surface of the water, wriggling and heavy and helpless on his own.

* * * *

WHEN THE sunlight has slipped almost to the top of the doorframe, Arthur looks at Husha in a hard, unrelenting way, a rigidity in the angle of his eyebrows, and says, I know you wanted more. I know you want more.

Husha shifts her weight from one foot to the other because her hip has begun to ache. More from what? she asks. Her arms are still crossed. From this summer? From you?

Hm, says Arthur. He shimmies his shoulders deeper into the water. Maybe. Although I'm not sure what more I or the summer could offer you. He shakes his head. No, no, he says. What I'm referring to is the book—your mother. I'm sure you expected more.

Husha shrugs. She looks up, away from him, and locates the sunlight on the ceiling.

You won't get it, says Arthur. You never would, not with her. Her silence, even after dying, isn't coincidental; it's not that there was something we missed, a letter or voice recording that was accidentally disposed of. You're lucky to even have the book. It *was* accidental, maybe, that she forgot to get rid of the book.

So you've decided, then, says Husha. There's no part of you that believes her death wasn't on purpose.

It'll always be a possibility, says Arthur. But, on purpose or not, intentional or not, you'll never get more than this. And even if you did, you wouldn't know her. Even if you had a book with every thought that went through her head from the moment her brain was developed enough to have conscious thought. Knowing someone's thoughts isn't the same as knowing someone. Not really, we can't—

He holds his chin up suddenly, draws his lips down, as if to curb a word before it reaches his mouth, perhaps a sob, a wordless sound that would reveal more than he wants to show her. We can't know someone even if they tell us all that they are thinking, he continues. This is something you must come to understand, or you will always feel disconnected from the people around you, you will always feel misunderstood, half-loved. It will always be a half knowing, we will always only have a half knowledge of each other. But this doesn't mean we must experience a half loving, or that the love we've been given was incomplete. Knowing someone and loving them are not the same thing. You won't learn to love your mother by knowing her better.

I do love my mother, Husha says. I already love my mother. I loved my mother.

Arthur scoops his lips up once more toward his nose. His earlobes wobble a little as he shakes his head again. We're always half-hidden, he says, even from ourselves. It's camouflage, it's necessity. Think of the cicadas. How else would they make it through the summer?

Sometimes, says Husha, but she doesn't finish her sentence. Sometimes, she wants to say, I wish you would shut up about the cicadas.

They're everywhere, he would have said.

And a reply, from him or her, inevitably one of them: They get into everything.

* * * *

TELL US a story.

Nellie reclines on the couch and looks at Husha with a glassy spark in the center of her pupils, a glint from the light withdrawing outside the window. Beneath her eyes are purple swipes of shadow, deepened in the evening hue of the living room. She hasn't been sleeping well, neither of them has, talking in the living room or in bed past midnight, long after Arthur has retreated to his room. They have a circling conversation, always the same, sometimes Husha thinks she can see it weaving in a figure eight, dust motes swaying in the dark air above their heads. It's the second half of summer now, the weather already leaning down into fall. A swell of rain often taps at the windows in the morning, allowing the residual chill of night to linger. A translucent fog smothers the lake until noon. When will Nellie leave? How long will Husha stay? Nellie will always be leaving, Husha senses, for the rest of her life. This isn't my home, Nellie says simply, lipless in the dark. And it isn't my mother who died. Nellie isn't cruel but explanatory, sensible. Husha senses that Nellie will always be arriving unaccountably on gravel driveways in the forest, her bag hiked up on one shoulder, shrugging off any surprise she encounters, the suggestion that her presence was ever unexpected. She will always be arriving unaccountably or leaving suddenly, in some stage of the process of departure.

August evening presses at the windows, humid with a back-slap of chill.

Tell us a story, Nellie says.

Arthur blinks, coming out of a stupor. He's been sitting in his chair since finishing dinner, and his body has molded to the rounded scoop of its back. He nods, head poking out between hunched shoulders.

Your own story would be nice, if you have one, he says.

Husha slips the grocery receipt they have been using as a bookmark back into her mother's book and crosses her arms. They haven't started reading yet this evening, have only just lit the candle and poured themselves drinks. Nellie and Husha have only just settled into their places and made themselves comfortable.

If I wanted to tell a story, I would have gone ahead and told one, says Husha, but her voice is open, conversational, contains no sharp edges.

I thought maybe you were waiting for the right moment, says Nellie.

I don't need prodding—if that's your insinuation.

You always need prodding, says Nellie. Husha hears, *To do anything, to go anywhere, to leave anything behind.* Husha, Nellie senses, will always be staying too long in one place, simmering, wallowing, for the rest of her life. And, Nellie continues aloud, I prefer the word *implication. Insinuation* feels nasty, unkind.

Well? says Husha, lifting an eyebrow.

Nellie rolls her eyes. Oh, come on, she says. Don't be so sensitive. I'm only asking if there's anything you want to add. Insight on the author, maybe? She was your mom, after all.

And his daughter, says Husha, ducking her head at her grandfather.

Mm, hums Arthur in assent. His eyes remain closed.

And I never met her, says Nellie. That's what I'm talking about. I thought I would learn more from the stories in the book, but—she's given me nothing, no details.

No explanation, thinks Husha. No clarification, no rationale. She thinks of the phone call, the peanut butter curdling under her tongue. It's fiction, she says.

I understand that, sighs Nellie.

And like you always tell me, it's not—

—my mother who died.

Right, says Husha, feeling a hole—gnawing, hollow, doubtful—at the bottom of her stomach. She shakes her head. I don't have any stories, she says. But part of her hesitates, flinches like flesh in response to pain. She's being honest—no stories have arisen in acknowledgment of, or in reply to, those in her mother's book. Husha understands how and from where her mother extracted certain details—the cottage country setting in "Homogeneous Nothing," for example, and the interactions between parent and child in "Mouth"—but these are obvious observations and certainly don't count as narratives worth relating. What have arisen, however, are images, disconnected flashes, splotches of color against the backs of her eyes. Considering Nellie and her grandfather both told stories from their own lives—however hyperbolic they may have been, she thinks, remembering El in the farm field, hair flying, and the group of squealing girls in roller skates—how would her images—arbitrary, indiscriminate—incorporate into the whole? When the images were violent, crude, and disjointed, where could they fit?

Nothing? asks Nellie. Nothing at all?

Nothing, says Husha. She wants to say, Nothing but what might count as end matter, nothing but fragment, figment, nothing but stringy leftover bits of nightmare, flimsy like snake skins dangling, nothing but acid reflux of the mind, a kind of gut reaction to the continual process of sitting down with her mother's words—nothing but a psychosomatic residue, thick on her skin, between her teeth, and sloshing inside her head.

She turns and looks toward the window. Nothing, nothing, she says.

* * * *

IN THE dislocated joint of her mind, in the emptied socket, Husha sees herself sitting in the forest behind the house. The cicadas are loud around her. The trees grow above her head into the sky. Her legs are spread wide. Between them, she curls her fingers and scrapes dirt toward her crotch. The earth is warm and vital, vibrating like fizz beneath her fingernails. As she scrapes and scrapes and scrapes and scrapes, the texture of the ground beneath her hands changes. It's soft and pliant, uniform, cohesive. She looks down to see that the soil has turned to skin, she has unearthed a face staring upward like a moon against a dark sky, gouges along its cheeks like long, pink tearstains where her fingernails tore. The face opens its lips, but its mouth is full of dirt. Husha watches the dirt shift as the tongue moves inside of it. She fights an impulse to plunge her fingers into the warm, saliva-coated cavity of the mouth.

The face's eyes, when they open, are nearly opaque, like marbles filled with smoke. They twitch in Husha's direction. They are her mother's eyes, it's her mother's face, of course, at the end of things, the end of everything, after all.

* * * *

IN THE dislocated joint, in the emptied socket of her mind, Husha picks her nose and discovers something nestled there. It's stiff and pointed, sharp against the soft pad of her finger. She shoves two fingers into her left nostril and grips and pulls—

and slowly, slowly extracts a thorn, a stem, leaves, petals, velvety, rouge, an entire rose garden from her face.

* * * *

IN THE emptied socket, Husha jumps into a lake and finds herself falling from a cliff underwater, falling up toward the surface and the air.

* * * *

IN HER dislocation, in the emptied socket of her mind, Husha stands in a hospital room and sees a woman lying on a bed, knees up, face turned to the side. She's naked beneath her gown, and Husha can see her exposed vulva, the compressed cushion of her bottom against the bed. She's pregnant, Husha realizes, belly huge—she's giving birth. And she's in pain, solidly, a constant moan vibrating from her throat. She's giving birth, in pain, the lights are bright and stark like an elongated lightning strike filling the room. She's alone and giving birth. She moans. Husha watches the woman's vaginal opening stretch, something white and round emerging, something knuckled, which unravels into a hand. The woman pushes, moaning, until the hand becomes an arm that grips its way across the end of the bed, wrapping around the mattress, becoming a shoulder lodged deep in the woman's womb.

* * * *

IN THE dislocated joint of her mind, Husha sees a frog floating belly-up in water, long legs extended, small, swiveling eyes—as small as fish eggs—dotting each toe on its feet.

* * * *

In her emptied, dislocated mind, Husha pulls apart a fig with her fingers (it's tough and muscular, like a miniature organ) and finds a living wasp inside.

* * * *

In the jointless socket of her mind, Husha walks through an abandoned house with slanted ceilings and wet cement floors. In the basement in the corner is a sleeping bag that turns over but has no body inside of it.

* * * *

In the dislocated joint of her mind, in the emptied socket, Husha wakes up in her mother's bedroom, in her mother's bed, coddled warmth around her legs, the night dense like winter slush, shadowy window adjacent. Unhurried, she senses that this moment will expand on and on, and reaches for the book that she knows like a boulder lies beside her.

Earth (Dirt)

SHE REARS OVER THE TOILET, wishing she could vomit, feeling as swollen as a rhinoceros, her belly as full of stretched-leather skin, radiating pain from the middle, the deep of herself, her thighs, surely, must be spilling over the toilet seat, wanting to rip apart and roar.

Surely there should be roaring. Bellowing. Something.

Surely something besides the sound of dripping, the occasional rush and splash of two liquids colliding.

She's imagining, once again, the tilt of Daniel's forehead, the gentle (was this too kind a word?) swoop, the downward (she must be kind to keep him, his sensitiveness) slope of his chin. She's imagining, again, the effectiveness of this tilt and this slope on the face of a baby. Convincing herself this would make for an effective baby face. That the baby would look gentle and sensitive and not some other synonym for these words. That the baby would replicate the best parts of them, the segments of herself and of him from which she didn't have to shrink (that mole behind his left earlobe, the long stubble that he missed or more probably neglected on his Adam's apple), that the baby would confuse the notion of her own singularity, that it would make her split and through fragmentation teach her how to recognize something outside of herself. Which was the same, she knew, as loving.

She admitted this once, to Daniel, to whom the act came so naturally, so imperfectly and intimately—*I don't know how to love.*

The baby is a splinter now, is scraping down the insides of her body. Seventeen weeks of growth sliding out of her into the toilet. She imagines the tilt of the forehead, the same tilt and size, perhaps, as the soft inside of her thumb. She thinks of Daniel, whose forehead at one time was the same tilt and size inside his mother's body, and his father before him, inside his grandmother.

At this moment, her manager knocks on the door. Adelaide, she asks, how long do you think you'll be?

Adelaide looks up through her sweat (she must be kind; she must speak kindly, to keep this job). Surely there are customers waiting.

One minute, she says. Curbs a moan. She reaches for her bag to find a pad to put in her underwear. She'll swamp herself, her jeans, to keep this job.

When she stands, she has to hold her mouth in her palm before looking into the toilet. Otherwise she feels her tongue might fall out.

The toilet water is black.

This isn't what she intended when she hoped the baby would split her.

Her hand hovers, she can't instigate the flush.

Adelaide— Her manager taps at the door.

In the fog of pain pulling up from the deep of herself, she takes her half-empty travel mug from her purse and dumps the coffee in the sink and dunks—

—and caps the lid.

Just washing my hands, she says through the door. Clean.

* * * *

SHE WASN'T always so hopeful.

Meaning, she didn't always root her life in hope, in faith (she didn't believe in God). In a baby.

She was a good student in high school, a good daughter. Her teachers told her with good grades that she was good. It became second nature for her to follow instructions (she must be kind, be sensitive, to keep her life, to carry it forth, to maintain it). Her mother told her with small nods of approval, small pats on the shoulder and smiles, small moments of freedom—you may go to the dance; you may stay out until midnight—small moments of trust, that she was good. And Daniel, when she met him in her first year of university, was so vulnerable she thought the relationship would break her, so liberal in his emotions, so tender, his hands pale and soft like night moths when he touched her, warm and careful, intimate like breath on her face. Good.

* * * *

SHE WAITS until Daniel is sleeping. The darkness hardens his face in silhouette against the window blinds, giving a form to his features that he doesn't otherwise possess. Her socks hiss on the hardwood stairs. In the kitchen, under the sink, a place where Daniel won't go digging, behind the cleaning supplies and the container for recycling, the drifting smell of disinfectant and stale beer, juice, is the travel mug, humming in its silence, feeling warm against her hand when she grabs it.

In the garage there is a sapling in a pot of soil. It's a theme—unintentional, instinctual. Have a baby, grow a garden. She bought the sapling on an impulse at Canadian Tire a week ago, holding her stomach while she stood in line, patting the flesh around her belly button. Something to care for. In the meantime.

In the strip of streetlight falling through the open garage door, the twiggy branches of the sapling wave like pliant bone.

The sapling is small. The hole Adelaide digs to hold its soil is shallow. She tips the travel mug and pours the contents into the earth, into the spaces between the knuckles of tree roots.

Ha-

She looks over her shoulder at the house. Lights off. Hush-hush of occasional and faraway traffic. Daniel is still sleeping. She turns and looks back and

loo

sees in the wash of streetlight a small something stuck in the tangle of roots. It could be a pebble, a bumpy peach pit, the severed, tilted tip of her thumb. It could be the start of a body, the sludge of melted limbs (the dark limbs of the grown trees framing the yard wave around her head), the messy idea of a skull, the size of a marble, a stone. The small something in the dirt is as unconscious as stone, as inanimate as stone. She feels a stone nestle like ice into her chest. She sticks a thumb—*thump*—against her sternum, the place where her ribs are sewn together.

Thump—to dig the cold stone, this ice cube inside of her, out? Impossible. Only to emphasize her own autonomy, this phrase that thumps to the beat of her thumb through her head: *I am I am I.*

Alone, she tucks the sapling into the dirt. On her way inside, she turns at the sound of what seems a faint whisper. A little

ha-loo

greeting, curling into the back of her ear. But perhaps it's only the whoosh of her brain tugging, telling her to go and get some sleep.

Before silence: the screen door whistling in the air. The crack of the wood back into its frame.

* * * *

Next morning, dipping his upper lip in coffee, Daniel wonders when she did the yard work.

Yesterday afternoon, says Adelaide. Before you got home. You didn't notice?

Daniel grunts.

You don't like it?

It's nice, he says, eyeing the tree.

I can change it, she says. Replant it.

I like it. How fast, he says, slurping, do you think it'll grow?

* * * *

She wasn't always so hopeful. She was hardworking. There's a difference. A difference between optimism and acts of duty. She graduated from university with a master's degree in media and communications studies. (She was thirty-two thousand dollars in debt; she must be kind—) Her thesis compared the cultural significance of fast-food commercials in childhood to the related trauma of witnessing slaughterhouse footage in adulthood. Her argument centered on nostalgia as a motivator for unethical consumption, nurtured through homely McDonald's ads. How many of our actions—how much of our lives, she wondered—are determined by our desire to crawl back into our smaller selves?

Six months after graduating, she landed a job as an administrative assistant at a naturopathic clinic, but only because the owner of the clinic was a friend of a friend of her mother's. It paid fifteen dollars an hour with a nearly full-time schedule. No benefits, no vacation days. Her peers from the media and communications program told her she was lucky. They were unemployed, still, some living at home with their parents. Many had started the PhD less out of desperation than disorientation.

Spending her evenings watching Netflix with Daniel and her weekends napping by her mother's pool, or lounging in her mother's hot tub, depending on the season, Adelaide forgot the sharpness of argument and the inflexible structure of well-crafted prose that she had become so familiar with in graduate school. She began to slip out of vegetarianism every time it became an imposition. It was a comfortable, almost cozy thing to do. Daniel decidedly had no opinion on animal cruelty. And when Adelaide came to visit, her mother was happy to no longer alter her cooking. Which she had been doing, out of respect.

* * * *

ADELAIDE TAKES to sitting out on the lawn after her shift at the clinic and before Daniel gets home from work. The sapling bends slightly in the wind, like a ballerina stretching backward. Recent conversations float through Adelaide's mind like radio stations sliding in and out of focus.

—so sorry, I'm so sorry, I'm—oh god, is there anything I can do? Just tell me and I'll do it.

—had two myself, before bringing you to term.

—Adelaide. This is a bit—well. You could have told me you were pregnant.

—you need to go to the hospital? I'll call—

—common for women who
start trying later in life. Not
that you're old.

—and you—you must—
be asking for time off?

—try again. Like right
away.

—ten to twenty percent of
pregnancies, actually.

—can spare you for
Monday and Tuesday, but
not much more.

—stupid of me to cry?

—my fertility doctor, if he's
still around. It could be an
easy fix.

—oh, Adelaide.

She crosses her legs and wrings her hands in the grass. This
time she won't tell them. Her hand floats near her belly button, as if conjuring, conducting. There is already a *this time*,
another pregnancy, despite her doctor warning her to wait.

What did he say? Daniel asked when she got home from the
appointment. Adelaide did not repeat the doctor's instructions:
Rest, it may feel like you're grieving a loved one. Wait at least
one menstrual cycle. Pay attention to your body, watch for fever,
excessive bleeding. Instead, she found herself presenting the word
fluke as an excuse. *Random. Inexplicable.* Holding the words out
to Daniel like bricks piled in her hands. A barrier scaling upward
to block her from the banal, *It's not my fault, I did everything I
should have done, the man can be infertile, too, you know—and
I'm not that old.* This, she reminded herself, was true: she had only

just graduated from university, was not yet nearing thirty. It was an irrational fear, ancient and yet premature, that made her think, *I'm not that close to death, yet. I can produce more than dead things.*

No, she won't tell them this time. The memories of their responses have begun to masquerade as her own thoughts, a garbled confluence of inward conversation.

—so sorry. (*I'm* so sorry.)—God—(Is there anything I can do?) —had two myself. (It's common for women.)—not that old. —is a bit—(We'll try again.)—can spare—not much. (Is it stupid of me to cry?)

But she hasn't cried yet, hasn't yet gathered the cloud of herself enough to cry. Which is problematic because (she hooks her fingers in the grass) this is when she feels she should most ground herself, hold herself inward as herself and herself alone. Repeat the mantra, *I am I am I.*

Which is problematic because (she hooks her fingers, smooths her fingertips across the earth) her edges have begun to fur and grow fainter, to grow fuzz.

Which is problematic because (she hooks and smooths and grounds her hands and didn't she do everything she should have done—didn't she follow instructions?) a sandwiching of opinions, deviant and undisciplined, unattached, has begun to swallow her throat.

* * * *

A BRUSH before silence, in the yard, in the absence of Adelaide. The sapling twists in the wind:

Ha-loo.

Look up at sky. Deep blueberry sky. Stretch limbs.

How far to reach deep blueberry sky?

Maybe be a blueberry bush.

Would like to—bear fruit.

Maybe be a blue canopy, arch over.

Stretch limbs.

* * * *

AT HOME, it's easier to transfer the contents of the toilet, still black, the stone at the bottom as big this time (there is already a *this time*) as a rodent, a hamster, she imagines small but long teeth and wonders if she should call an ambulance, her mother, she was sitting for hours in the bathroom, her pubic bones beginning to ache on the ceramic, her lower back and stomach grinding—easier now, this time, much easier to transfer the contents of the toilet to the backyard.

She uses a plastic bucket that she finds under the sink.

And plants the second sapling close enough to touch branches with the first. To mingle roots.

Ha-loo?

Haaw-looow.

The saplings touch and

Ha-

sing.

loo.

Haaw-looow.

Brittle creak. Can hear great, brittle—

Been stretching.

Been growing? Deep blueberry sky. Maybe be—

Oval lilac sky.

Maybe be oval lilac today.

Will stretch, then. Will stretch, too. Nothing—

Nothing else to do.

With nothing else to do but stroke the sky with words and grow, pain themselves skyward, the voices slip like time. Time like water over stones, smoothing the rough edges of rock and breaking silt with their toes. They watch Adelaide come and go. In five months, there is another tree, the dirt around its base turned up, turned into lumps and fluffy. In eleven months, another.

Ha-

Haaw-

loo.

looow.

Hay-

Hell-

lew.

laaw.

Daniel sees the scars of blood along the toilet bowl but doesn't know (the gentle swoop of his forehead, the slope of his chin) what to say. He sinks into the silence scooping like a bird with heavy wings around the house, gets caught in the undercurrent of air that hums out from Adelaide's body (his sensitiveness, vulnerability, vibrates there). When she asks him to make love to her, he does; and cleans the toilet bowl with the same precise, rhythmic pulses.

He admires the trees in the yard, the gradual increase in their height like a family standing at attention. Adelaide's fastidious determination in planting them is (fanatic) impressive—her scheduled and (obsessive) unceasing care for them admirable.

Ha-loo.

Haaw-looow.

Hay-lew.

Hell-laaw.

Adelaide takes to sitting out on the lawn when she's supposed to be at work. She will lose her job—her manager, apologetic, calling her through the phone—she will lose her job somewhere soon along the way. She takes to sitting out on the lawn where Daniel can see her. She likes the trees to see her.

See her watching?

Always see her watching.

Why won't she leave alone?

She likes to hear them speak of her.

Why do think she put here?

Why do think she plant here?

Why?

Think she tore out on purpose, to place here. Think she knew this is a better place, a softer place and darker. Think she knew this place has veins stronger than inside her. Turn the dirt and have roots. Turn the dirt, the earth, look beneath and the trees are holding feet like holding hands. Turn over, turn her inside out and she's alone and sprinkled with capillaries. Turn her inside out and still there's muscle before the bone. Think she meant to turn out, lead here. Churn under in red and rot and discharge foam.

Maybe if stretch, grow fruitish, touch and be painted by blueberry sky.

Disintegrate?

Can't feel hooks of thought anymore, can't feel the separate claws of root.

Oval lilac sky.

Oval disc sky. Dislocated spine of sky.

Maybe she put here to stretch, maybe that's why.

Adelaide, in response, thinks—now, as she flushes the final body from her body, the final replication of her body from her body, from the bathroom looking out to the yard, she thinks Maybe I—

Have I misstepped, misspoken? Was there some growth too heavy for me here, some weight I've failed to hold? Have I mis-carried?

Did I carry you incorrectly? She looks toward the toilet bowl. If you can be a you. And I an I. Perhaps I held my breath too long between the syllables of that mantra, a miscalculation the size of the gap between two microscopic heartbeats: *I am I am I*. Was it the blending of this and you that did the hurt? *I am you am I*. Misappropriation. Misuse of pronouns. Here, somewhere here in the *I* comes the heart of the confusion.

Did *I mis-carry* you?

She scoops the bucket from the toilet and carries it into the yard. Carries it steady, carries it. The grass is cool on her feet. She folds, her haunches touching the earth. This will be the last. The last planting. She unplants from inside herself compulsive re-creation (and will she be unkind? Undedicate herself to the cultivation of that swoop and slope? The swollen curve of a belly expanding. The delicate roundness of parenthetical thoughts).

Will her brain (break free from bracketing?) retract its tendrils from the needless and thick, oily, composted, deoxygenated earth?

She looks at the trees. She will tend them.

She touches the bark, the wooden wrinkles, the baby leaves.

She rests her hands in her lap. Doesn't see the blood and dirt between the ridges of the spirals of her fingertips. Doesn't see this detail, doesn't notice and doesn't know, doesn't need to duplicate, she feels the wind coming softly through the trees, a careful splitting in the fibers of her hair, a splinter at the roots.

HUSHA AND NELLIE LIE beside each other in the bed. Husha's hair, which is longer than Nellie's, lies across her shoulder and the crook of Nellie's arm. The curtains are closed and it's dark and silent in the room—the cicada song is absent like the absence of rain striking a window after storm. The two women fidget minutely in their sleep, fingers occasionally twitching, eyes jumping beneath eyelids.

They dream.

* * *

IN THIS dreaming they are buried deep underground like babies in a womb, legs tangled together like tree roots.

* * *

HUSHA AND Nellie don't argue anymore or have conversations deep into the night. All of it is tired. All of it is old.

They begin a different bedtime routine. First, Nellie puts her hands in Husha's hair and kisses the top of her head. Then the tip of her nose. Then both sides of her jawbone. Then the place where her collarbones meet, then the bottom edges of each rib cage. Then the hips where they protrude, the kneecaps, the ankles—joints swelling gently against skin—the heels, the bottoms of the feet.

* * *

IT TOOK Husha a long time to love Nellie, or to admit that she loved Nellie. And it wasn't only because Nellie was a woman.

206

It had more to do with force and possession—more precisely, a lack of force and possession in the way Nellie acted toward her. Nellie wasn't jealous, didn't ask offhandedly, *Who are you texting? Where are you going? Who are you going to see?* Unlike most of the men Husha had been with, Nellie's flirting wasn't rimmed with venom. When Husha said, *I think I'll go home now*, she didn't reply, *Maybe I won't let you*, falsely playful, or the guilt-invoking response, *But you just got here.* At worst Nellie would look her over, state simply, *I wish you would stay.*

Husha was friends with Nellie first—they had met in her master's program at the University of Toronto—and she assumed she could only, physiologically, as part of her genetic makeup, love Nellie platonically. So, when she sensed this lack of force and possession—a patience and democracy she seldom discovered in men and therefore didn't recognize as love—she didn't remove herself, didn't think to pull away. This is what she knew good friendships to be: gentle and polyamorous, careful, loyal but without paranoia, unsuspicious. Friendship functioned with less interpersonal control, and less conceit. Husha found that she could spend time with many people as friends that she would never dare to be with sexually or romantically for fear of social repercussion. Love—deep love—had always been the same to her as emotional occupation, a form of identity-building, like a person collecting artifacts with which they fill the shelves of their home. A partner, a lover, becomes a part of you much like the clothes you wear, the food you eat, the places you choose to go or not to go, how and where you earn and spend your money. And just as each person selects these habits and adornments for a particular purpose—for status or comfort or political statement or rebellion or self-protection or self-preservation—so too does each person select their partner, and so too must they manage this new extension of themselves that wanders, disturbingly, autonomously, apart from them through the world.

Husha has come to understand that this need for control in love is narcissism, insecurity, but for a long time she accepted it as care. She accepted it as compassion. Throughout her childhood, Husha's mother had authority but few regulations, had been uncontrolling almost to the point of inattention. Home late from work and rarely concerned about where her daughter had been, what she had been up to, Husha's mother granted her child radical independence. She herself, of course, was radically independent, husbandless and introverted, almost antisocial. She was straightforward and efficient, leaving the house clean, the refrigerator stocked with food, her daughter prepared for school and signed up for her preferred extracurricular activities. Birthday presents were bought. Carpooling was arranged. Husha's mother cared for her, she took care with detail. But Husha was lonely. She watched movies and read books and listened to songs on the radio, and everywhere around her—in the ads on TV and up close in her friends' families—were people, she felt, who were actually happy, who really loved each other, who fussed over one another, who probed and bickered and prescribed change. People who—claustrophobically or not— were physically and psychologically present.

Husha, arriving home every day after school to an empty house, to the well-organized rooms and vacuumed rugs, the windows without smudges—what she felt to be more a manufactured replica of a home, a hollow exhibit, than the real thing—believed that the Disney films had it right. In her mind, she skirted around the ache of what was missing in her life. She convinced herself that love was ownership—what else was that epitome of love, marriage, but that ownership in legal terms, publicly proclaimed? She convinced herself that love was to be entangled with another person, to reflect and define them. To be reflected and to be defined. Surely, to be with someone intensely and for a long time was to step into a rhythm not unlike a repeated echo in an enclosed space. Husha felt but could not put into words the competition inherent in that drive for definition (who decides the tone and timbre of the note reverberating off the walls of that relationship?), each person struggling to lay claim like a colonist to their own self-discovery that by necessity must involve another life, bound up, neatly categorized, and explicable.

Love to Husha became proprietorial, combative. And this—precisely this—was what induced attraction and arousal. She felt a violence and a conquering at the brink of sexual encounters. A feverish conflict as her body met another's, ecstatic subjugation. Nudity was feigned vulnerability: passion's prerequisite was attack. Love of another meant invasion.

Nellie, when she arrived in Husha's life, taught her a different kind of submission. A submission of herself to herself. Like cutting a monster across its throat, Husha left something bleeding and frothing, infected, behind her each time she took to Nellie's body with her hands.

* * * *

HUSHA WAITS until Arthur is out in the garden in the afternoon, she waits until he begins to whistle and his hands are in the earth, and then she goes into his bedroom and opens the box.

She's careful not to bend or tear the cardboard flaps. She's careful to memorize how the flaps were folded together so she can replicate their design. She doubts her grandfather would notice a change, but she's careful nonetheless. She turns her body as she kneels on the floor, one ear tilted toward the door, so she can hear if he comes inside. She feels sinister, something bubbly and nauseous at the top of her chest—she thinks of her grandfather lying in bed and asking how long Nellie would be staying with them, asking without accusation, without demands or a need for explanation, the protective looping of his arm around the box in the basement, the worried lines striping his forehead— but she can't help herself. She feels hungry and mutinous, can't hold back.

The box is full. Husha takes each item into her hands and then places it on the floor, forming a long line beside Arthur's bed. She makes a mental inventory, knowing this might be her only chance to view the contents of the box. The more objects she places on the floor, the more she wonders if her grandfather might not have been mistaken: maybe there's another box in the basement that he meant to bring upstairs instead of this one. The objects mean nothing to Husha. They could belong to anybody. She sees no pattern or importance and eventually gives up, breathing hard, placing the items one by one back into the box and folding the flaps closed.

* * * *

THREE WHITE taper candles.
A framed picture of a cartoon apple.
A comb with no hair in its teeth.
A small, chunky Spanish-to-English dictionary.

Blue nail polish.

A stuffed gray elephant with a missing back leg.

Four matchboxes. (Husha moves them beside the taper candles.)

A Snakes and Ladders boardgame.

Two *Cottage Life* magazines with various pages ripped out.

A black-and-yellow disposable camera.

A drill with a rubber handle.

Eight metal screws, two bolts.

A tall, white mug with the sketch of a mushroom on one side.

An open box of plastic spoons.

A lightbulb wrapped in a dishcloth.

Chapstick.

Five permanent markers of different colors (black, brown, red, dark green, yellow), dried out.

An empty sketchbook, priced at one dollar, twenty-five cents from Dollarama.

A pair of pink tweezers.

Two (stretched and gummy, dusty) cotton balls.

A dog collar without a tag.

A package of glow-in-the-dark stars.

* * * *

TELL ME about her, says Nellie.

They're sitting out by her grandfather's garden in the dark, on the single concrete step leading down into the grass. A long rectangle of light from the sliding glass door behind them throws itself over their shoulders and onto the ground, illuminating the edges of plants and dimpling the earth with shadows. Everything in the garden is wilted, limp, leaning over.

It isn't tulip season, but Arthur tucked the bulbs into the dirt regardless, hoping the cooling borders of the day would trick the flowers into thinking that it's springtime. The stiff tongues of their leaves have begun to push halfheartedly out of the soil.

Husha and Nellie don't have to whisper out here as they do in the living room with Arthur sleeping down the hall. Every window is closed, Arthur could never hear them, but still their voices never rise above a murmur, and in this way their words mix with the low sounds of the water down the hill.

What do you want to know? asks Husha. She has a hollow feeling in her throat, like the dip before a cough.

Nellie shrugs. She nudges Husha with the side of her body. Knocks their kneecaps together.

Husha pulls her lips between her teeth. Nellie watches her for a moment from the side of her eye, a sliding of pupil toward the drooped corners of her eyelids. Every feature of her face is relaxed, almost morose, as the darkness of the evening hangs around them, slinking up to and swallowing the side of the house. The outlines of trees fifteen feet in front of them are hazy, here and there the suggestion of pockmarked bark, the swell of roots up against the earth. Nellie sighs.

Something, she says. Tell me something.

Husha stares without expression toward the trees. I don't know, she says. She says it with purpose, perplexed, a high sound hitching up almost like a yelp into her voice. Or a hiccup. In that moment, in moments like this, she believes she knows nothing, that she can't remember a single thing about her mother.

There, in her memory, is someone taking her to the park, pushing her on the swing. It isn't her mother, it can't be—the woman doesn't have a face. There's a blank space, a gap of solid air, between the woman's wrists and Husha's body, where palms should meet and press her lower back, propel the swing forward toward the opposite end of its arc.

The swing swings back and Husha is whiplashed into another memory: she's young, maybe ten years old, receiving a bowl of tomato soup so hot that pain flashes brightly through the skin of each of her fingertips. The soup is passed across the table in the kitchen of the house where she grew up. The soup is passed by a tall person who wears vague clothing, maybe a pair of jeans, maybe a loose, knitted sweater, dark in color, maybe. The soup is passed by arms that belong to this tall, faceless person, this woman, elbows straightened, leaning over, reach extended, hair falling across a collarbone. Husha takes the bowl. Where their fingers might brush, the woman's fingers disappear, abruptly lopped away. Husha places the soup down on the table, pretends the bowl didn't burn her, and reaches for her spoon. The smell of tomatoes meets her nose and tunnels down her nostrils to the back of her throat. On the refrigerator somewhere to the left are photographs pinned with magnets. In one photograph, Husha smiles with a faceless woman crouching beside her, their shoulders touching. Physical contact—here, look, confirmed!—in a memory of a memory. Proof of her mother's physical existence has leaked past the barriers of Husha's conscious mind. Husha raises a spoonful of soup from the bowl, a spoonful that she is certain will blister her tongue—she turns her head toward the kitchen door and the hallway beyond, which is dark, climbing with darkness, like fog or smoke blooming up toward the ceiling (and what is that she sees at the end of the dark hallway, motionless against the wall?).

She turns her head toward the kitchen door and she is overcome, she's older, but still young, preteen, rushing out of dance class with her backpack pulled over one shoulder, an SUV waiting for her by the curb, a faceless woman in the driver's seat with her hands wrapped, tense, around the steering wheel. Snowflakes dot her knuckles like freckles, her own, Husha's, not the woman's, her own knuckles hooked around the backpack strap as she shortens the distance between herself and the SUV, the invitation of the empty passenger seat.

She opens the door to the vehicle and she is opening the door to a hospital room, a faceless woman lying half-conscious on the bed. (What did the doctors do to her face? Where did it go? What effect did the meds have? What color were the eyes? Who misplaced the nose?) In an adjacent cubicle partitioned off by a curtain that doesn't quite reach the floor, a TV blares loudly. Maybe it's showing the morning news, maybe it's the weather channel. Maybe the woman has feet at the ends of her legs, maybe she doesn't, maybe she doesn't have shins because when Husha reaches out to touch her body where it lies beneath the bedsheet, she feels these parts, the resistance of bones and muscle beneath her hands, but if she lifted the sheets—which she doesn't, which she won't—she knows the woman's limbs would be invisible or cut away. If she focuses too hard on the memory, the bedsheets will deflate and flatten beneath her hand. She's a teenager in this hospital room, uncertain how to behave, inexperienced, unsure what to ask for or what to expect. Later, after multiple visits of a similar nature, she will understand protocol, follow procedure. For now she feels small and finds the washroom so she can retch dryly into the sink and then raise her head to look at herself in the mirror, a head not quite faceless but blurry, smudged around, the idea of a nose in the middle, two divots suggesting eyes, the dark dash of eyebrows, the hollow gap of mouth.

If she opens her blurry mouth too wide, she's older and sobbing into her hands, sobbing her whole stomach out into them. She's cupping her face in her hands so that her face stays on her face and doesn't slip away. If she closes her eyes too tightly in the cupped palms of her hands, the eyelids smooth over and thicken, her eyes seal shut.

Nellie, on the back step, knocks their kneecaps together. The tulip bulbs sit locked in the earth, in shadow.

Something, she says again.

I don't know, says Husha. In that moment, in moments like this, she has convinced herself that she can't remember anything.

Nellie exhales. Anything, she says. The stupid things, the small things. What was her favorite color?

Husha hesitates. She would have thought it useless for a person to choose a favorite color, she says.

Nellie is silent for half a second and then crunches her eyebrows down toward her eyes, tosses up her hands. Enough, she says. Bullshit. Don't be difficult.

Husha blinks. She says, I suppose she wore a lot of green.

What kind of food did she eat? asks Nellie.

Small portions, says Husha. Vegetables, mushrooms—pickled eggs, slowly, in little slices, like they were a delicacy.

What did she do in the evenings?

Laundry. Books. TV.

What were her pet peeves? asks Nellie. Did she have any surgeries, any scars? Allergies? What made her nervous?

Husha answers each question automatically, numbly, her voice jumping out of her mouth like a knee bucking up beneath a doctor's tentative hammer, testing for reflex. She leans in closer toward Nellie, works to regulate her breathing. Doesn't venture too far into thought.

* * * *

WHEN NELLIE takes the book and splits it open with her fingers and opens her mouth to speak, Husha leans over and covers Nellie's lips with her thumb, her palm against her jaw. Arthur pretends not to see. Husha pushes and meets no resistance, her thumb swallowed into the warmth of Nellie's saliva. She wants to kiss her then, fully and without concern, scoot their bodies together and wrap her legs around her spine, but she resists out of respect for her grandfather. Nellie's eyes soften and her tongue moves around her mouth.

It's the last story, says Husha. Mind if I read?

Nellie sucks at Husha's thumb as she slides it free.

Husha takes the book and pulls air into her lungs. She steadies herself and counts in her head, like a diver counting before executing a particularly difficult twist: one, two, three.

Doll Face

The Bad Thing, *what her mother said*

Her mother hadn't gone easily like people dying of cancer do
in movies. Brain tumors are different. They split and push and
shift things around between the ears. Madeline was alone with
her mother in the hospital room when her mother said what she
said. This is all Madeline will tell the therapist sitting across
from her in his office chair, face patient like wood and drawn,
hands folded, nodding.

Her mother had not gone easily.

This is all she will tell him. She won't say anything more.

The Purple-Stained, Half-Chewed Popsicle Stick

It clings to and dangles from her father's bottom lip. His beard
and mustache are stubbly. He's gotten back into sweets since her
mother died, doughnuts from the neighborhood bakery, Ben &
Jerry's ice cream, Sour Patch Kids in crinkly plastic bags, Pop-
sicles on hot days like this one. His tongue, which dashes out to
scoop around his teeth, is dark blue. It's early morning, the sun
still sends shadows leaning far out from the bottoms of trees.
Madeline is fairly certain her father hasn't eaten breakfast, only
the Popsicle.

Madeline closes her eyes and turns her face toward the car
window. She feels a headache swelling up above the roof of her

mouth. Today marks one month since her mother's death and none of them could sleep, not Madeline, not her father, not her younger sister, Gemma. They stayed up late playing cards and watching old Disney movies, lolling around the living-room floor in pajamas until the sun rose. Her father suggested pancakes, but the girls weren't hungry. He left for a while, making noises in the kitchen, and then came back with the Popsicle in his mouth and phone in hand, waving the screen in front of their faces, flashing an address, before telling them to get in the car.

The morning mist outside is sticky on the road like cotton. Gemma huffs about having to sit in the backseat—she's thirteen now and should, she articulates, have equal rights to the front passenger seat. Her expression in the rearview mirror is as rumpled as her pajama pants, the knees of which she lifts and fits under her chin.

The Yard Sale(s)

It was something they did on weekends with their mother when they were younger, Madeline and Gemma each gripping a handful of toonies as they moved up and down the stranger's driveway. A treasure each: they were allowed one treasure each, which they bargained for like professionals. Their mother laughed, watching. She set careful watching lines on them with her eyes.

When the girls were finished, their mother would buy something for herself, something useful like a clean, white lampshade or uncreased oven mittens. Madeline remembered her moving up and down the driveway this way that way as if through fog, touching and holding things this way that way with her long fingers and strong palms.

Madeline, Gemma, and her mother were back in the car and home before her dad was up and dragging himself through the kitchen with gray sleep slinking out from beneath his eyes.

The Deep Something

Madeline could feel a deep something in her belly when she breathed.

A deep something sadness. She could feel a deep something in her throat that groaned up to her lips, tried to tunnel through her teeth. She could feel a deep deep inside of her that plowed through small talk, what her grade ten teachers said to her at school, her friends a distance away in text messages on a cell phone.

She could feel the plowing through of small loves inside of her. How she used to like rain in the leaves of trees, cool like wet fingertips in her hair; how she used to read books and fold the page corners; how she had tadpoles in a tank when she was little and watched them grow into frogs. How she released them back to the pond. How she and her sister used to watch movies in bed with her dad's iPad, ears pressed together, eating snacks from the variety store down the road. Madeline liked Shirley Temples, the bubbles and the little sword through the maraschino cherry; Madeline liked the sound of wind outside the house in the evening—*Can you hear the dark, shifting howl?* her mother would whisper.

She felt all this pulling apart slow like cotton candy inside of her. She could feel a deep something beneath all the small loves like cold rocks in her toes.

The Sewing Machine

It's black and heavy and shines like obsidian in its box. It's pricey, a Singer antique, but her father doesn't care. In fact, he insists. And Madeline doesn't object because she knows this purchase will make him feel at ease on the day one month after her mother died, buying something real and formidable for his daughter, something she can use with her hands.

Madeline takes the round metal skull of the machine between her fingers.

Gemma, wandering in her pajamas near the end of the driveway, begins to whine and says she wants pancakes after all.

Her father says she can't speak like that and expect the front seat in the car. He rumples her hair.

The woman running the yard sale collects the money from Madeline's father and boxes the machine and shuffles it into Madeline's arms.

The Original Bill of Sale, taped to the inside of the box

Madeline holds it up against her father's nose. The two of them are blurry from an early morning nap on the couch and armchair in the living room, post–yard sale. It will be a long Sunday. Her father is watching TV.

What? he says, cross-eyed, looking at the yellow paper.

She pushes it closer. Is it Mom's name? she asks.

Her father sits up and takes the paper and his eyes run all over the page. Nineteen-fifty-three, he mumbles. He squints and skin gathers up like a little mountain between his eyebrows.

Okay, he says. He looks up at her. The TV is making laughing sounds in the background. His mouth is concerned: From that old sewing machine, huh?

Madeline nods.

Joan Adams, he says, was your great-grandmother's name. She was ancient when I first met her. Died a few years before you were born. Your mom's dad's mother. Your grandfather's mom.

Madeline can't put it together. She says, So the "Bill of Sale" means—

That the sewing machine belonged to your great-grandmother. That she was the first to buy it from the store, to own it. The "Bill of Sale" is like a receipt. It's a legal document.

Ownership, says Madeline.

Yes, says her father, steepling an eyebrow and leaning back into the couch. He hands the paper back to her. He's tired and his chin moves down toward his throat.

But what, says Madeline, moving into his sight line, putting herself back into his attention, does it mean?

Her father tilts his head. They listen for a moment to the TV and Gemma puttering out in the kitchen. Madeline's fingertips have become damp and smudgy on the paper.

Her father turns his voice sweetly when he speaks: Do you believe in ghosts?

The Inheritance

Later at dinner, at the table as the sun falls through the back window, he says, Maybe it's your inheritance.

The Fabric and the Thread

Madeline pulls out the fabric and the thread that the woman from the garage sale stuffed in the box beside the sewing machine. The two pieces of fabric are folded, soft fleece, one piece purple, the other muted cream. Small swatches, enough to make maybe a pillowcase, maybe a long hat, a pair of mittens, a couple of headbands. Madeline pulls the fabric to her nose and breathes in. Her nostrils draw microscopic smells: mud crusted between rubber treads of boots, the warm, dark inside of a cat ear, hay leaning against a wall of old barnwood, heavy rainfall on asphalt shingles, a wet snail belly peeled from the earth.

Madeline moves her fingers this way that way through the fibers.

The thread is black, one spool.

She winds the thread around her knuckles. She doesn't know how to sew, but she has an idea of how it works. When she was little and her grandmother was still alive (and her mother, for that matter—she imagines them, all these dead women marching in a line backward through her personal history, herself a living and continuing component of this line), her family would go to her grandmother's house for Sunday dinner. After eating, Gemma would head outside to play in the grass with the dog and her father would trail behind to watch with a beer in his hand, one hip leaning against the back porch railing. Inside, Madeline would sit on the carpet in the living room with her mother on the couch and watch her grandmother sew. She didn't know how, herself, but she had an idea, a loose conception, of how the separate actions of threading the needle, aligning the fabric, and animating the machine came together to form the whole, the unit, the stitched creation.

Above the whir of the machine the women would chat inconsequentially, in the slow, tumbling way of Sunday evening conversations.

I found a new lasagna recipe, her mother might say, absently twisting her hair through her fingers. (Madeline, in her bedroom, in recollection, twists the thread.)

I like mine just fine, her grandmother might say, maneuvering the fabric, the chug-chug-chug of the machine on the table. (In recollection, Madeline must remind herself that this sewing machine on her grandmother's table is not the same as the one in the box in front her—this one once belonged to her *great*-grandmother. Again she watches the dead women marching backward.)

Too much garlic, her mother might say.

Differing taste buds, her grandmother might retort.

Anyway.

Yes, anyway. I took Dot to the vet, her grandmother might

say next. (Madeline digs up this name Dot from her memory, the old Yorkie dog rolling out in the grass with Gemma.) She's going blind. Cataracts.

Or she might say—

I've started a new television show, a crime documentary.

Or—

They say there'll be a storm tomorrow afternoon. One of those good summer storms.

On it might go, the machine chug-chug-chugging and Madeline leaning back into her wrists.

Madeline watched in those moments but did not do, did not speak or sew, waiting in the held-breath patience of children hoping to have some secret unveiled by the older crowd, feeling like an imposter, accidentally admitted into the closed space of casual adult speech. She continues the practice of observation now as she opens her laptop and pulls up YouTube, spending the yawning length of Sunday afternoon streaming how-to videos on Singer sewing machines, feeling clumsy and ill-equipped, untrained. She heaves the machine clunking from its box. Through the floor rises the sound of the TV murmuring, and Madeline imagines that her father has fallen once more to sleep. The rest of the house fogs dreamlike around her as she falls into the digital image of a woman's hands running fabric through the machine on her screen.

Madeline huffs and sucks her lips into her mouth. The machine in front of her is as arresting and unfamiliar as a wild horse. She identifies the motor, the sloping, black arm, the cornered, metal face plate, and the narrow foot. She winds the bobbin with black thread, locks it onto the post beneath the throat plate, and places the spool on the spool post. She follows the video, using a thread guide to thread the needle, rotating her hands through the broad throat space beneath the arm. When she turns on the machine, the parts move together as one, startlingly quick and precise, puncturing.

Gemma hears the noise and comes into the room slowly like coming out of a dream. She sinks onto the edge of the bed and draws up her shoulders to the sides of her jaw.

What will you make for me? she asks.

Madeline laughs and shrugs and sets her eyes on the purple and cream fabric that she pins together like layers of skin beneath her hands.

The Doll

In two hours she has made a terrible something with two eyes, two arms, two legs, but no mouth. It has a cream-colored body, crudely naked, and a purple face. She stuffs it with cotton balls she finds in the bathroom cabinet and ties black thread around its scalp for hair. Gemma, who has fallen asleep sideways on the bed, shifts awake to clap halfheartedly at the creation.

Madeline looks down at the mouthless face, at the terrible something the day has birthed. Sunlight out the window finds its groove and moves down the sky. Terribly something she has made with the machine and her hands.

The Hands

The dream is drained of color like vision after staring into the sun. The house is bright and beige but full of long shadows unraveling down the upstairs hallway. Deep from the walls comes the sound of a dog barking, sharp, yapping hiccups that wedge themselves solidly into the air. Madeline stands in her bedroom doorway. Behind her is her bedroom and Gemma's body, curled up on the bed and sighing quietly in sleep. In front of her is the hallway and the top of the staircase yawning. At the end of the hallway, cut out of the quietness of the house behind the dog barking, is the half-open door to her parents' bedroom.

Madeline leaves the soft, nosing sounds of Gemma sleeping and moves her limbs over the hardwood floor, socks gliding. Her arms are light at her sides as if they have been caught in an invisible air current, vibrations humming darkly between her ears, the opposite of gravity under her armpits. She smooths her feet in butter steps along the floor and approaches the half-open door.

Madeline knocks the door forward with her forehead.

A hush kicks out the back of her throat. The room is dark, a milky hue at its edges. Through a swab of blue translucent window light, Madeline sees two lumps lying in the bed in the center of the room. Blankets envelop. The lumps rise and fall, breathing. The dog yaps louder somewhere deep in the wall to the right. Madeline turns and finds the closet and opens its slatted door. Smothered beneath old clothes the dog is yapping and rummaging. Madeline kneels and shifts the clothing aside, feeling dust like little moth wings moving up into her nose, and finds instead of a dog something hairless and bony. The thing dislodges itself from the fabric, wrestling a T-shirt off its back, and Madeline sees that it's a hand, dismembered, two fingers raised like antennae or spears. A long, low whine that is no longer a bark emanates from the creased wrinkles in its palm.

Madeline heaves herself backward and discovers that the bedroom door is closed. She reaches for the handle. Thick flesh presses against the metal—her hands are gone, her arms end in sealed, swollen mounds of skin. Behind her, the dog-hand wails from the closet. She turns and the room has changed, something, one of the blanketed lumps is sitting up on her mother's side of the bed. It has a tangle of thin, black hair around its head. It has pockets in its head that might be eyes but no mouth (the other lump lies quietly); it has a long white body that shuffles out from under the blankets, cushioned and naked, Madeline feels a wailing build up like storm clouds, like wordlessness inside her head—

—its face is purple and stitched onto its body.

—it stands, wavering.

Madeline puts her hands up to cover her eyes and finds herself fingerless.

The Shutting Mouth

Breakfast the next day is quiet. Morning hangs over Madeline, Gemma, and their father like a limp umbrella, the rest of the day leaking ahead. Madeline hasn't slept much and exhaustion hitches up like a tingling shadow, pressure, the concussive aftershock of impact behind her eyes. Gemma's hair falls around her face and shoulders as she crunches cereal. She still hasn't changed from her Saturday-night pajamas, but there's a bounce to her jaw as she eats that suggests choice in this matter of clothing and getting dressed. There's a roundness to her cheeks, a wholeness to her shape and expression that implies energy, balance, control. Madeline feels the raw edges of herself curling up. Her father floods cream into his coffee and takes his seat at the table. His skin is still blooming rouge from his morning shower.

Need a ride to your appointment after school, Madeline? he asks, lifting the coffee mug to his lips.

The unspoken word—*therapy*—passes through them like piano wire threading through their ears. They each attend separate sessions with the same doctor, have been going since their mother's diagnosis, a result of her insistence that they talk to someone other than each other. But Madeline attends more frequently than her father and sister, once a week. This was decided after the nurse rushed in to find Madeline trying to pull the machines from her mother's body, wrestling with her half-conscious mother on the day she died.

No, says Madeline, a croak escaping with her voice. She coughs. I'll walk, thanks.

You sure?

I'm sure.

Gemma crunches. Her father drags at the coffee with his lips. He watches Madeline bring a spoonful of milk and granola to her mouth.

You'll have to show me that sewing machine later, he says. You managed to set it up?

Madeline swallows. Sure, I managed, she says.

She made something, says Gemma. A doll.

Madeline feels the backs of her hands go warm, heat seeping down into her nail beds.

A doll, says her father. I'd love to see.

I didn't make anything, says Madeline. She tucks the metal spoon between her teeth and bites down.

Yes, you did, says Gemma, I saw—

Oh, it doesn't matter, says her father quickly.

But it's true, says Gemma.

Madeline releases the spoon and tastes a metallic, icy sting gather in her saliva. Do you ever just shut up? she says. Do you ever just for one second shut your fucking mouth?

The Black Cushioned Chair

Sure, says the therapist, sitting upright with his notebook. His hair is slicked back and shiny, black as the chair Madeline sits on. Sure, I could answer that question, but first I think you should try. It's been a month now since your mother died—

Over a month, says Madeline.

Okay. Over a month since she died. Have you changed?

Since she died?

Yes. That was your question, not mine.

So maybe you should be the one to answer it. I thought it was your job to answer questions like that.

Madeline pinches back a burning sensation in her eyes and looks at the long, rectangular windows, the steepled ceiling, and the bookshelves that line the walls. She looks at the lamp shedding dull light on the black cushioned chair.

The therapist watches her with a level gaze.

Okay, he says. To be honest, I'm not sure if you've changed. To be honest, I'm not sure if it matters.

How would that not matter?

I'm just not sure if that's the best way to measure things.

Through change? I'm here to get better.

Are you? You started coming to these sessions before anything had really happened—I don't mean emotionally, of course. But you started coming *in preparation* for what would happen. Your visits with me have never been to just "get better," but to reduce suffering before it arrives. To build understanding. Of the world, of death, of yourself. Or at least to chip away at your need for understanding. Your time here isn't just to right what has gone wrong—if *wrong* is even a word we should use in this situation.

My mother was dying.

Yes. It was difficult. It *is* difficult. But it isn't—necessarily— wrong. This is explainable death, the kind of death we have time to register and come to terms with. Mothers are supposed to, someday, die. It's happened earlier than you expected, okay. So let's work on and work through the surprise of it all. What I'm saying is that this is maybe more a matter of perspective than progression.

A matter of perspective.

I don't think we have to, if we don't want to, buy into the notion of constant betterment, of healing unbroken things, mending things that aren't torn. Do you see what I mean?

Madeline's mouth is tight across her face. But you said I should work through it, she says. Doesn't "working through" something mean that you move past it, beyond it? It implies progression.

Maybe that's it, then, says the therapist. Our language is limited. Our established phraseology—ah, how should I put this?—our words, our syntax, the way that we are bound to piece our sentences together, convinces us we must go forward, must go on, must leave something behind as an obvious consequence of linear living.

Madeline stares blankly at him.

He says, If the only words we have available to us describe progression, then how can we imagine otherwise?

Madeline shifts in the chair. You don't think I've changed, she says.

The therapist sighs. He drops his voice. Maybe, he says, this would be a good time to tell me about the day your mother died. I've heard what happened after, of course, from your father.

And if it's all a matter of perspective—

Madeline—

No, she says. She laces her fingers together in her lap. There are some sacred things that reach up behind words but never grasp them by their lettered edges. Some sacred sloping that must not be linguistically touched and fondled. Some unsearched moments must remain.

You never answered, says the therapist. Do you think you've changed?

Madeline cannot say.

The Needle

She had put the doll facedown in her sock-and-underwear drawer, but now she takes it out and holds it by one leg, rotating it, the skinny thread hairs waving downward. She sits on her bed while evening collects itself behind the window blinds.

Downstairs her father is shuffling pots and pans in the kitchen, prepping dinner. Gemma, she knows—she just passed her on her way upstairs—is in the living room doing homework on her lap. The furnace thrums deep down in the basement. The house begins its gradual descent and tumble into the end of the day.

Madeline smooths the thread hairs down onto her thigh. The mute, purple face of the doll looks up at her.

This doll has a different kind of mouth, she thinks. Different from a human, a person, herself, her mother. Or it would, if she made a mouth for it, if she wanted it to speak. The mouth would be a rip in an already complete composition, a wreckage of wholeness, continuity. Do not shred this fabric into fragments, she thinks. Do not scatter the parts. Do not title them. This is not an arm—she holds up a small, rounded doll arm. And this is not a leg or a body—she lifts the leg and torso. This is not a head or hair or a face—she rolls the little head in her hands, inspecting the threaded eyes.

With her own eyes she looks up at the old machine, the sewing mechanism heavy on her desk across the room. In her belly she feels this heaviness; her neck has turned to stone. Do not shred this, do not scatter, she thinks, and raises her body from the bed. She knows now how to dislodge the needle from its mechanical hug. The thread she must guide out of the machine and shift back through the needle. The needle clamp she must loosen. In the mirror her mouth is open slightly like a cabinet door. She positions the needle under her upper lip and locks her thumb to its base.

She forces the needle upward and the skin of her upper lip

parts with a small popping sound like a bug snapping dead against a car windshield.

Silent, Madeline pulls the thread through.

Through, working through her flesh, segmenting these two lips of skin together, she turns the needle and hooks back the way she came.

ON THE AFTERNOON NELLIE tells Husha that she's leaving, she hauls groceries onto the kitchen counter in a plastic bag that stretches at the bottom, and wrestles a peach from the bag's depths. The peach has clearly been bumped around, bruises patterning its skin in gray patches smaller than thumbprints. Nellie holds the peach aloft in one hand. She looks thoughtful. She doesn't say anything, holds her tongue.

Husha wonders if Nellie is teasing her, if this moment is intentional or contrived, the peach with its pit hidden beneath the firm layer of the fruit, much like the peach that in Husha's mouth tasted like sunshine or at least forgetfulness as she sat by the driveway that first morning.

Arthur, from where he naps down the hall in his bedroom with the door open, makes small animal sounds—he coos like a cat purring. These sounds toss themselves like vacant thoughts into the kitchen. It's midafternoon and the light outside the window behind Nellie, which frames her, seems not to have changed since midmorning. There's a frozen quality to the day, a staleness, like an old photograph.

Nellie holds the bruised peach aloft in one hand, examines it. She looks thoughtful and doesn't look over at Husha and doesn't say anything. A heat moves up from Husha's stomach and expands across her chest. Something is beating under her tongue, thrumming against the soft space between her lower jawbones like a small and struggling bug, like an insect dragging and slapping its wings through saliva. She imagines a cicada crawling out now from between her lips. She imagines catching its thorax between her teeth. She imagines—clamping down.

Husha swallows and finds the inside of her mouth dry.

Arthur hiccups down the hall, still asleep, and swallows in turn. A sound like lips smacking somersaults out of the bedroom doorway.

Husha wonders if Nellie is mocking her, teasing, as she examines and rotates the peach—wonders if she even remembers that Husha held a peach pit in her mouth that morning as Nellie approached. Wonders most of all if it matters, the precision of Nellie's memory of that morning.

Nellie rotates the peach with precision until she lands on an unbruised portion, then she leans forward, her elbow on the countertop, and sinks her teeth in.

At last, releasing the words like a held breath, she speaks.

* * * *

ON THE evening after the afternoon Nellie tells Husha that she's leaving, Husha hears a dog barking outside—distant—and follows the sound into the forest.

She's sitting on the edge of her bed, midway through putting on her pajamas, when she hears it. She pulls up her red-checkered PJ shorts and goes immediately into and down the hallway and then out the front door. Arthur and Nellie, sitting in the living room, see but do not follow her. They don't give a sign, neither a motion of approval nor a questioning look, that suggests whether they have also heard the dog barking. Outside beyond the yellow porch light, the driveway and forest are dark. The air smells mossy and solid, wet, like impending rain. The sound of the dog barking is low and insistent, yes, distant, and only audible because the cicadas' screaming has fallen off along with the afternoon heat. The resounding silence is thunderous, and Husha can hear each displacement of stone as her bare feet step down into the gravel.

It's possible that the dog belongs to a neighbor whose cottage is down the driveway and across Curry Road, by the bigger lake. It's possible, but then the dog is lost and far from home: the barking, she now realizes, comes from the other side of the house. She's gone out through the wrong door, and so she wanders through the gravel, along the side of the house, and around the back to the garden. The barking comes from down the hill, from the forest beside the lake.

Husha moves down into the trees.

It's possible the dog has wandered up from the marina, where cottagers often walk their dogs. In the forest Husha feels leaves, pine needles, and the sharp edges of thin, fallen branches against the bottoms of her feet. It would be a far journey from the marina, even for a dog, and so Husha knows that the dog is lost and has misplaced, or been misplaced by, its owner. Husha can't decide if the barking denotes fear or aggression. Either, both. The forest is impenetrably dark, and if she were to turn, Husha wouldn't be able to see the light anymore from the house behind her up the hill. The sound of the dog barking ricochets off each tree trunk and claps into her ears. It's possible the dog is not a dog at all.

Husha walks until her feet hit mud, cool and squeezing up between her toes, and then water and reeds sliding across her shins and the backs of her thighs. She turns again to the left, into the forest and the sound of the dog barking, and has many near misses with low-hanging branches and is cold up to her knees from the drying lake water.

* * * *

LATER INTO the night after the afternoon Nellie tells Husha that she's leaving, Nellie sits on the back step by the garden. She laces her fingers together as if tying a sturdy knot, places them between her knees, and waits for Husha to emerge damp with lake water, sweat on her skin, dusted with dirt and pieces of leaves, the smell of midnight in her undone hair. She waits for Husha to emerge like clarity, first imprecise and shadowy, sharpening with each step forward, materializing and becoming material—emerging steadily in this way from the forest.

* * * *

EVEN LATER now into the night, or early into the morning, after the afternoon Nellie tells Husha that she's leaving, the two women go inside the back door and move in tandem down the hall to the bedroom. They close the door behind them and don't turn on the lights.

In the gray static of the bedroom, Husha thinks of sight, which turned black and impossible while she walked in the forest. Now, in the bedroom, she thinks of sight, remembers the summer in sight (her mother on the steel coroner's table, the skin of her neck): Nellie down by the lake, pushing her long toes into the sand; dead cicadas in clusters just outside the front door in the morning as if they had been anxious, in their final blurred moments, to get inside; Arthur with his hand clamped around the refrigerator door handle, attempting but unable to open it, his nagging hunger and a confused desperation evident in the torquing muscles of his wrist; the liver-spotted, loose skin on the back of his hand; the sun tilting down into the trees, or up through the trunks, the seesaw of the sun each day and its interaction with the landscape, that give and take of shadow; the slow, wide cavity of her own mouth as she yawned into the bathroom mirror in the morning or night, preparing for or closing the day; the sharp, yelping colors of fruit in a bowl on the kitchen counter—red, orange, yellow, dark blue.

Husha thinks of smell, remembers the summer in smell (the pansies and lilies, the funeral home parlor): the damp scent of broccoli steaming on the stovetop; Windex on paper towel, then mirror glass; the bake of driveway gravel in the afternoon; a foggy remnant of Nellie's bodywash lifting up from the underside of her jaw—

Husha blinks, closes her eyes as she and Nellie close the bedroom door behind them, and thinks of sound, remembers the summer in sound (the dog barking like a hammer against the air, like ripping paper, in the forest): the shhh-shhh-shush of her grandfather's feet down the length of the hallway; the mumble of lapping water at the lake's edge; the thunder-drum of the shower hitting the ceramic bathtub; the lack of alarm clocks in the morning; Nellie's voice leaning over with her mouth across the top of the couch while Husha lay below, Nellie's voice on the top of her head, in her hair; Arthur reading from her mother's book in hushed tones, stumbling over certain sentences, readjusting his magnifier in his lap, quiet cursing; Nellie reading from Husha's mother's book; herself reading from the book; the cicadas, the cicadas, the cicadas.

When Husha thinks of cicadas, she thinks of midday, the

time when they're loudest, hurling their song out of the trees, and, in this way, when she thinks of cicadas, she also thinks of sunlight—the cicadas but also the sunlight has begun to get everywhere, get into everything, leaking through the vibration of insect wings that Husha feels always against her eyelids, inside her ears. For now maybe it's enough to not question the cicadas' arrival in the trees around the house or claim understanding, for now it's enough to not stop the push of the cicada song through the windows and walls, for now it's enough not to describe or dissect. The whirring of wings will someday cease or persist, either way. Without wonder or worry she can carry on either way.

And along with the cicadas and sunlight, Nellie—

When Husha thinks of cicadas, she thinks of the dead insect that worked its way into the cereal box, she thinks of a dead cicada working its way into her mouth. She thinks of her tongue and the papery texture of her gums, the ridges along the roof of her mouth as she and Nellie close the door behind them. She thinks of taste, remembers the summer in taste (peanut butter toast suctioned to the back of her tongue): the metallic edge of the water from the kitchen tap; the metallic edge of vanilla ice cream licked off spoons; the salty and leathery aftertaste of Arthur's skin the few times she kissed him while helping him into bed; soup from the stove, sucked off her finger that she dipped in to test the temperature; smoke from the extinguished candle forming flavor in her mouth; sticky saliva in the inside pockets of her cheeks, post–afternoon nap; something, some substance that she will not name, that she would not, previously, name, as pulpy and warm as comfort rolling off her lips as she pulls—

Erica McKeen

—her hands down the sides of Nellie's torso, along her ribs and descending below her hips. They've closed the bedroom door behind them. Touch—she would not, previously, think in touch, remember her summer in touch (her mother who, in pandemic lockdown, she could not touch, could not reach): the whorled peach pit in her mouth; the ache of incorrect posture in her spine, curled up on the couch in the evening; the pinch of her bra along her sternum; sweat gathering along her hairline; summer heat from sunlight coming in the kitchen window; summer heat inside the sunbaked car; summer heat by the lake, in the bedroom at night, throwing aside the blankets; the soft down of Nellie's hair in her hands, between her fingers—

Moving—

Now—

Down—

And descending below her hips, the door to the bedroom closed behind them in the late night or early morning after the afternoon Nellie tells Husha that she's leaving. Husha's hair is a tangle down her back, still clotted with leaves from the forest, as Nellie guides her onto the bed. Nellie's hair, in a simple braid, hangs loose around her ears. Husha's clothing—her PJ shorts and old T-shirt—clump and are cold in Nellie's hands, but her skin is warm, gritty with a film of leftover sweat, and malleable: moving the fabric of her clothing aside, Nellie finds no resistance between Husha's legs. A wideness or width, expansiveness in the angle of her thighs as she draws Nellie in closer, holds her secure—a welcoming, a beckoning, but most of all, or most notable to Nellie, who didn't believe the conversation was finished when Husha left the kitchen that afternoon, a yielding to the pressure of Nellie's hand.

The yielding of Husha's body, urgent and responsive, prompts Nellie to hoist herself onto the bed, anchoring her hand between Husha's legs, the flat of her palm hard against Husha's pelvic bone, and press her mouth into Husha's ear. She moves against her, a clock ticks high up on the wall, the silence of the early morning, still in darkness, pushes at the window. They hear a night wind, slow, against the side of the house. Nellie's breath rushes out hard into Husha's ear when Husha loops her forearms around the back of Nellie's neck. Oh God, says Nellie, the words slipping, warm. Husha releases a huff, a gasping, in return. Oh God, says Nellie, come with me. It's what she wanted to say in the kitchen but didn't. Her mouth against Husha's ear: Come with me. Come home with me. Leave with me. She moves her hand slowly, spreading her fingers. The braid unwinds from her hair. Come with me.

Husha, remembering the warmth expanding up to her neck in the kitchen as Nellie leaned into the peach, feels the warmth from between her legs move up to her stomach, her breasts, down her arms. She's warm and soft, every part of her body like dough; her bones are no doubt bendable, she feels the weight of Nellie's body above hers, the insistence in her voice. Husha is water, falls apart in Nellie's hands, against the palm of Nellie's hand between her legs, her joints dislodge from their sockets. Her body relents: Come with me. But she says nothing, a whir-ring a shushing fills her mouth along with a rush of saliva. She is silence, a bidding to. Come with me, in her ear. Her body, screeching like a bird into open air, relents. She sets her jaw, silent, and shakes. The useless word swallows up her head: *Stay.*

Come with me, once more in her ear.

Husha wraps her hands around the back of Nellie's skull, turns her head, feels each vertebra of the spinal column in her neck turning, kisses her, and comes, her body bursting like a headache against Nellie's hand.

CAN YOU HEAR THAT? asks Husha the next morning, leaning out the back door.

Hear what? Nellie rubs sleep from her eyes and places her chin on the back of Husha's shoulder. I don't hear anything, she says.

Husha breathes in through her nose. They're gone, she says, her voice giant in the silence reverberating.

Together they look out at the edgeless gray sky framing their field of vision.

By MID-AUGUST, the cicadas have been dead for more than a week. Soon their eggs will hatch, and the liquid-white bodies of the nymphs will drag themselves in armies to the earth. Birdsong arrives in the absence of cicadas screaming in the trees. Owls in the evening, loons from the larger lake, woodpeckers slamming their skulls. Even the wind is audible—even the thrum of a hummingbird skirting the shingled edge of the roof.

Muffled like a choke, inside the house is the sound of Nellie lifting each piece of clothing that belongs to her from the dresser, folding it, and placing it in her bag.

* * * *

HERE WE are at the end now, and Husha is sitting down by the lake.

Here we are now and Husha sits in silence.

Nothing cushions the space behind her back except open air. No clock ticks high up on the wall, no clock winds down. Nothing is hampered by measurement here.

Husha doesn't think her stillness, sitting down by the lake, is stagnation, inertia. The frozen moment after the clock winds down isn't indecision. The clock doesn't choose whether to tick or not to tick, whether to keep going or to hang back. Husha doesn't choose her name, but nevertheless she is silence, or at least a bidding to; she is stillness, immobility, blunt exhaustion contorting beyond its limits and procuring a quality of meditation. Husha feels, sitting down by the lake, drugged, serene, soft, toothless. She sees stones nudging their way microscopically into the ground. She sees the tips of water weeds interrupting the lake's surface and plunging unabashed into open air. She sees the tail of a squirrel lounging over a high tree branch and, beyond the branch, pinpricks of orange sunlight laughing between leaves. Can clarity blur and still be called clarity? She reaches down to hold her toes in her hands. She can feel the ridge of each callus on the soles of her feet. The lens of her mind gathers mist in the same moment it rotates into focus.

Here we are now and Husha looks unwavering across the lake.

Nellie is no longer behind her, up the hill and in the house. Husha feels the fact of Nellie's absence in her body more than she knows it in her head. It's fine. Husha reminds herself that this absence is fine, that they agreed to it, after a time, after talking and talking it out: an expected departure strategically placed just before the boredom and tedium of cohabitation set in. They finished her mother's book, didn't they? And found no stalwart admission at its conclusion. No proclamation of pending suicide, no grand explanations or assurances, no peace, no secret notes. No map, literal or figurative, of how it all goes together.

They finished her mother's book, but even if they hadn't, Husha believes that Nellie would have left. Everyone, after a time, grows tired of telling stories.

Besides—Nellie's departure was not only expected but unavoidable, without escape. Summer is ending, after all; there's money to be made. Not everyone can mooch off their dead mother's inheritance and live indefinitely in cottage country (Nellie's words, with a demure edge to her expression—they both know that no one would want to, that no one would give up their mother for this). After dropping Nellie off at the bus station in town—after watching her walk across the bus bay, her body leaning to one side to counterbalance the weight of her bag, her hair already coming out of its braid—Husha drove home and sat in the driveway for a long time, staring heavily through the windshield at everything she doesn't have to pay for.

Then she went down to the lake.

Water clutches muddy at the back of her throat when she looks at the lake. It's like looking at lightning across a vast field, or the vacuum of an arctic galaxy: cosmic, sublime, wholly otherworldly, and yet at the same time an event deep within the body—momentous, skeletal. She sits in the weeds and watches the water lick the shore (small winds, light like confetti, drift and move the air around, displace water, shove it up against the sand) and wonders—if this lake were an ocean, would it roll inside her head and make her interpret the world differently, think things blue or slow or tumbling like tidal currents? Would life feel heavier somehow, rounder and more assured, if this lake were an ocean? Would the rhythm of the tide serve as a better metaphor, a more suitable context, than this shrinking lake? Would Nellie's leaving seem a part of some natural process of crowding in close and timely receding? Husha wonders about the way in which the atmosphere funnels the direction of events, shapes conclusions, consciousness. The buildings around us, she now believes, prop up the architecture of our minds.

Husha hikes her legs up to her chest and hugs her knees close to her body, dragging her heels through the sand. As she thinks of the ocean, she notices darkness settling in the trees across the lake. She thinks of the ocean and imagines it rising up around her, tucking into her ears, sea snails moving up her nostrils, crabs prying at her lips. She imagines Nellie inside her head, or perhaps just behind her left shoulder, saying, *What's this about oceans? Don't you know where you are?*

Husha has seen the ocean once, on a trip to Halifax with her mother. She looked out at it and found it empty. The air was cold and sharp and, later, when they went back to their hotel room, there was salt on the hems of their pant legs from where they had stepped down into the water. They sat on the end of the bed in the hotel room and looked out at the city through the wide, almost ceiling-to-floor window. The light was steely coming into the room. They had come to Halifax to visit some relatives of Husha's father whom she'd never met before. Tomorrow they would go for brunch. Husha felt as if she had wandered into an alien landscape, not because of the temperate climate or the seaside views but because she would be going to brunch—brunch!—with her mother in the morning and a group of strangers that her mother used to know intimately but didn't know at all anymore. They sat on the end of the bed and wondered if they should wash their hair before morning, get the grime of airplane travel out and replace it with shampoo. They were unused to speaking with each other casually now—Husha was twenty-one years old and hadn't lived with her mother in three years. The hotel room was cold and Husha rooted around in her suitcase on the floor for a pair of woolen socks, which she pulled onto her feet.

Hey, said her mother. She was still looking out the window and her face was turned away. Her arms looped softly around her abdomen, cupping her elbows. Hey, she said, we could go walking there again tomorrow, by the water, before heading out to eat. It wasn't bad walking there, was it? We'd have time, I think, before our reservation.

I think so, said Husha. Yeah, I think we'd have time.

Good, said her mother. It's good to have a little extra time.

Acknowledgments

Thank you to the literary journals that selected and published earlier versions of some of these stories: *Surely Magazine* (formerly *Shirley Magazine*) for publishing what is now titled "Swamp Woman"; *Perhappened Mag* for publishing "The Homogeneous Nothing"; *Long Con Magazine* for publishing "Mouth"; *The Dalhousie Review* for publishing "The Surfacing"; and *PRISM International* for publishing "Anne, Cassandra, and the Sleep House."

Thank you to my first readers and now disbanded workshop group, in particular to Kevin Andrew Heslop and Shelly Harder, who coaxed and nudged and questioned much of this writing in its early stages.

Thank you to my friend Rio Picollo, who tells the most bizarre and unaccountable true stories, some of which were the seeds for narratives and conversations in this book.

Thank you to my agents, Victoria Dillman and Carrie Howland; to my editor, Helen; and to the entire team at Norton.

Thank you lastly and most immeasurably to Tobi, for everything.

About the Author

Erica McKeen is a Canadian fiction writer. She is the author of two novels, *Tear* (Invisible Publishing, 2022) and *Cicada Summer* (W. W. Norton & Company, 2024). Her work has won the Rakuten Kobo Emerging Writer Prize, been chosen as a finalist for the ReLit Awards, and been selected as a *Globe and Mail* best book. Her stories have been published in numerous literary journals, including *PRISM international*, *filling Station*, and the *Dalhousie Review*, among others. She lives in Vancouver, British Columbia, where she works as a teacher and librarian.